There was only so much temptation a woman could resist.

They rode the last wave to the beach, tugged the boards up past the high water mark and left them there. Matt took her hand and led her up to the house and still no words needed to be spoken.

This was right, Kelly thought, a great wash of peace settling over her as her body tingled with anticipation of what was to come.

She'd come home.

That was a dumb thought. It was a thought that had to be shelved, and it was—because how could she think of anything but Matt leading her into the shower off his bedroom, Matt stepping into the shower with her.

She couldn't think past his body. The rippling muscles of his chest, the traces of sand in the hollows at his shoulder, the way the water ran from his smile right down to his feet. She could see every long, gorgeous inch of him. He was in the shower with her, and for this night, for now, every single thing in the world could be forgotten except that this was Matt and he was here, now, and for tonight he was hers.

Nothing else could matter.

Dear Reader

Last year I attended a writing retreat on Australia's famous Gold Coast. The world surfing championships were taking place five miles down the beach. Then the weather turned wild, so the championships were relocated—right into our sheltered bay, right under our hotel! You can imagine how our retreat ended. We hung out of the windows and watched gorgeous surfers from all over the world, 'hanging ten' just beneath us.

But I *was* there to write... Virtuously I took my laptop out onto the balcony and searched for inspiration. Strangely, it wasn't very far away.

I had fun on the Gold Coast, and I had fun writing this book. WAVES OF TEMPTATION lets me share that glorious surfing world, the inevitable medical needs of such an event, and the drama and passion that must inevitably lie beneath.

This is also my 100th romance novel. Writing for Mills & Boon® has been a wonderful journey. A huge thank you to all who've helped me along the way. And thank you to my writing friends and to my family.

Thank you, too, my readers, for sharing my passion.

Marion Lennox

WAVES OF TEMPTATION

BY
MARION LENNOX

Published in Great Britain 2014
by Mills & Boon, an imprint of Harlequin (UK) Limited,
Eton House, 18-24 Paradise Road, Richmond, Surrey, TW9 1SR

© 2014 Marion Lennox

ISBN: 978 0 263 24366 6

Harlequin (UK) Limited's policy is to use papers that are natural,
renewable and recyclable products and made from wood grown in
sustainable forests. The logging and manufacturing processes conform
to the legal environmental regulations of the country of origin.

Printed and bound in Great Britain
by CPI Antony Rowe, Chippenham, Wiltshire

Marion Lennox is a country girl, born on an Australian dairy farm. She moved on—mostly because the cows just weren't interested in her stories! Married to a 'very special doctor', Marion writes Mills & Boon® Medical Romances™, as well as for Mills & Boon® Cherish™. (She used a different name for each category for a while—if you're looking for her past Romances search for author Trisha David as well.) WAVES OF TEMPTATION is Marion Lennox's 100th romance novel.

In her non-writing life Marion cares for kids, cats, dogs, chooks and goldfish. She travels, she fights her rampant garden (she's losing) and her house dust (she's lost). Having spun in circles for the first part of her life, she's now stepped back from her 'other' career, which was teaching statistics at her local university. Finally she's reprioritised her life, figured out what's important and discovered the joys of deep baths, romance and chocolate. Preferably all at the same time!

Recent titles by Marion Lennox:

Mills & Boon® Medical Romance™

GOLD COAST ANGELS: A DOCTOR'S REDEMPTION*
MIRACLE ON KAIMOTU ISLAND†
THE SURGEON'S DOORSTEP BABY
SYDNEY HARBOUR HOSPITAL: LILY'S SCANDAL**
DYNAMITE DOC OR CHRISTMAS DAD?
THE DOCTOR AND THE RUNAWAY HEIRESS

*Gold Coast Angels
**Sydney Harbour Hospital
†Earthquake!

Mills & Boon® Cherish™

CHRISTMAS AT THE CASTLE
SPARKS FLY WITH THE BILLIONAIRE
A BRIDE FOR THE MAVERICK MILLIONAIRE*
HER OUTBACK RESCUER*
NIKKI AND THE LONE WOLF**
MARDIE AND THE CITY SURGEON**

*Journey through the Outback duet
**Banksia Bay miniseries

**These books are also available in eBook format
from www.millsandboon.co.uk**

DEDICATION
For Marion

Praise for
Marion Lennox:

WAVES OF TEMPTATION
is Marion Lennox's 100th Mills & Boon® novel!

PROLOGUE

SHE WAS HUDDLED as far from the receptionist in the funeral parlour as she could get. Curled into one of the reception area's plush chairs, she looked tiny, almost in a foetal position.

Her dirty, surf-blonded hair was matted and in desperate need of a cut. Her cut-off-at-the-thigh jeans were frayed, her too-big windcheater looked like something out of a charity bin and her bare feet were filthy. Her huge grey eyes were ringed with great dark shadows.

In ordinary circumstances, Matt Eveldene would have cast her a glance of sympathy. He might even have tossed her a few coins to get a decent meal.

Not now. Not this girl.

He knew as much about her as he'd ever want to know. Her name was Kelly Myers. No. Kelly Eveldene. She was seventeen years old and she was his brother's widow.

She rose as she saw him. She must know what he'd been doing—identifying for himself that the body lying in the funeral home's back room was indeed his brother's.

'I...I'm sorry,' she faltered, but she didn't approach him. Maybe his face stopped her. It was impossible to conceal his anger. The white-hot rage.

The waste...

He'd just seen Jessie. His beloved big brother. Jess,

who'd laughed with him, teased him, protected him from the worst of their father's bullying.

Jessie, who was now dead, aged all of twenty-four. Jessie, who for some crazy, unfathomable reason had married this girl two weeks before he'd died.

'How can you be married to him?' he snapped. It was a dumb thing to ask, maybe even cruel, but it was all he could think of. He knew so little of what Jessie had been doing for the last few years. No one did. 'You're only seventeen.'

'He wanted to marry me,' she said, almost as a ghost might talk. As if her voice was coming from a long way away. 'He insisted. He even found my father and made him give permission. I guess...my father's still my guardian, even if—' She broke off and sat down again, hard, as if all the strength had gone out of her.

But Matt had no room left in his head for pity. Not now. He'd loved his big brother. Jess had been wild, free, bordering on manic, but he'd lit their lives. Or he'd lit Matt's. In the big old mansion overlooking Sydney's famous Bondi Beach, with its air of repressed elegance and propriety, and its walls echoing with his father's displeasure, it had always been Jess who'd brought in life.

But that life had been more and more out of control. The last time Matt had seen him he'd been in a rehabilitation ward in West Sydney. Jess had been twenty-two. Matt had been eighteen, confused and desperately frightened at the state of his big brother.

'I can't go back home, Matt,' Jess had told him. 'I know what Dad thinks of me and it always makes it worse. The black dog...depression...well, when you're older maybe you'll understand what it is. When I get out of here I'm heading overseas. Following the surf. The surf gets me out of my head like nothing else can. If I'm to stay off the drugs, that's what I need.'

What had followed then had been two years of inter-mittent postcards, the occasional press clipping of minor success in surf competitions, and demands that his parents didn't try and contact him until he'd 'found' himself.

Had he found himself now, on a slab in a Hawaiian mortuary? Jess… He thought back to the last time he'd seen his brother, as a recovering addict. Recovery had been for nothing, and now he was facing this girl who was calling herself Jessie's wife.

His anger was almost uncontrollable. He wanted to haul up her sleeves to expose the tracks of the inevitable drug use, and then hurl her as far as he could throw her.

Somehow he held himself still. He daren't unleash his fury.

'He wanted to be cremated,' the girl whispered. 'He wants his ashes scattered off Diamond Head, when the surf's at its best. At sunset. He has friends…'

Matt bet he did. More like this girl. This…

No. He wasn't going to say it. He wasn't going to think it.

Married! His father was right—he needed to pay the money and get rid of her, fast. If his mother knew of her existence, she might even want to bring her home, and then the whole sad round would start again. *'Please go to rehab… Please get help. Please…'*

He was too young to face this. He was twenty years old but he felt barely more than a child. His father should be here, to vent his anger, to do what he'd ordered Matt to do. Matt felt sick and weary and helpless.

'Can you afford cremation?' he demanded. The girl—Kelly—shook her head. Her grey eyes were direct and honest, surprising him with their candour.

'No,' she replied, her voice as bleak as the death that surrounded them. 'I hoped… I hope you might help me.'

In what universe could he help a woman who'd watched his brother self-destruct? Even if she looked…

No, he told himself. Don't think about how she looks. Just get this over and get out of here.

'I'm taking my brother home,' he told her. 'My parents will bury him in Sydney.'

'Please—'

'No.' The sight of his brother's body was so recent and so raw he could barely speak. Dear God, Jess… He needed to be alone. He felt like the world was closing in on him, suffocating. How could his father demand this of him? This was killing him.

Maybe his father was punishing him, too. Punishing him for loving his big brother?

Enough. He had to leave. He hauled a chequebook from his jacket and started writing.

The girl sank back down into her chair, tucking her feet back under her, assuming once again that position of defence. Her eyes became blank.

The cheque written, he handed it to her. Or tried to. She didn't put out her hand and he was forced to drop it onto her grubby knee.

'My father had an insurance policy in my brother's name,' he said, struggling to hold back his distress. 'Even though we doubt the validity of your marriage, my father acknowledges that you may have a claim on it. This pre-empts that claim. This is the total value of the insurance policy, given to you on the condition that you make no contact with my parents, that you never attempt to tell my mother that Jess was married, that you keep yourself out of our lives, now and for ever. Is that clear?'

She didn't pick up the cheque. 'I would like to write to your mother,' she whispered.

'I can think of a hundred reasons why you shouldn't contact my mother,' he said grimly. 'The top one being she has had heartbreak enough and doesn't need to be lumbered with the mess you've made of your life as well. My father has decided not to tell her about the marriage and I understand why.'

She closed her eyes as if he'd struck her, and he found his fury fading.

This was unfair, he conceded. This girl was a mess, but, then, Jessie's life had been a mess, too. He didn't need to vent his grief solely on her—but he had to get out of there.

'Use the cheque,' he said. 'Get a life.'

'I don't want your cheque.'

'It's your cheque,' he said, anger surging again. 'It's nothing to do with me. All I want is for you—his *widow*—' and he gave the word his father's inflection, the inflection it deserved '—to sign the release for his body. Let me take him home.'

'He wouldn't have wanted—'

'He's dead,' he said flatly. 'We need to bury him. Surely my mother has rights, too.'

Her fingers had been clenched on her knees. Slowly they unclenched, but then, suddenly, she bent forward, holding her stomach, and her face lost any trace of remaining colour.

Shocked, he stooped, ready to catch her if she slumped, concerned despite himself, but in seconds she had herself under control again. And when she unbent and stared straight at him, she was controlled. Her eyes, barely twelve inches from his, were suddenly icy.

'Take him home, then. Give him to his mother.'

'Thank you.'

'I don't want your thanks. I want you to go away.'

Which fitted exactly with how he was feeling.

'Then we never need to see each other again. I wish you luck, Miss Myers,' he said stiffly. Dear God, he sounded like his father. He no longer felt like a child. He felt a hundred.

'I'm Kelly Eveldene.' It was a flash of unexpected fire and venom. 'I'm Mrs Eveldene to you. I'm Mrs Eveldene to the world."

'But not to my parents.'

'No,' she said, and she subsided again into misery. 'Jess wouldn't have wanted his mother hurt more than she has been. If you don't want to tell her, then don't.' Her face crumpled and he fought a crazy, irrational impulse to take her into his arms, to hold her, to comfort her as one might comfort a wounded child.

But this was no child. This girl was part of the group that had destroyed his brother. Drugs, surf, drugs, surf... It had been that way since Matt could remember.

Get out of here fast, he told himself. This girl has nothing to do with you. The cheque absolves you from all responsibility.

Wasn't that what his father had said?

'Sign the papers,' he told her roughly, rising to his feet with deliberation. 'And don't shoot the entire value of that cheque up your arm.'

She met his eyes again at that, and once again he saw fire.

'Go back to Australia,' she said flatly. 'I can see why Jessie ran.'

'It's nothing to do—'

'I'm not listening,' she snapped. 'I'll sign your papers. Go.'

Kelly sat where she was for a long time after Matt had left. The receptionist would like her gone. She could understand that, but she was the widow of the deceased. The funeral home would be repatriating the body to Australia. It'd be a nice little earner. It behoved the receptionist to be courteous, even if Kelly was messing with the décor.

She needed a wash. She conceded that, too. More, she needed a change of clothes, a feed and a sleep. About a month's sleep.

She was so tired she could scarcely move.

So tired…

The last few days had been appalling. She'd known Jess's depression had deepened but not this much, never this much. Still, when he'd disappeared she'd feared the worst, and the confirmation had been a nightmare. And now… She'd sat in this place waiting for so long…

Not for him, though. For his father. She hadn't expected a man who was scarcely older than she was.

Matt Eveldene. What sort of a name was Eveldene anyway?

A new one. She stared at the bright new ring on her finger, put there by Jess only weeks ago. 'You'll be safe now,' he'd told her. 'It's all I can do, but it should protect you.'

She'd known he was ill. She shouldn't have married him, but she'd been terrified, and he'd held her and she'd clung. But she hadn't been able to cling hard enough, and here she was, in this nightmare of a place.

She'd been here for almost twenty-four hours, waiting for whoever came as the representative of Jess's family. She knew they'd have to come here.

She had to ask.

'If ever something happens, will you scatter my ashes out to sea, babe?' Jess had asked her. Had that only been a week ago? It seemed like a year.

She'd failed at that, too. Matt had simply overridden her.

Like father, like son? Jess had told her of his bully of a father. She'd been gearing herself up to face Henry Eveldene, but Matt's arrival in his father's stead had thrown her.

She'd failed.

'I'm sorry,' she said to the closed door behind which Jessie's body lay. 'I'm so sorry, Jess.'

There was nothing more she could do.

She rose and took a deep breath, trying to figure how to find the strength to walk outside, catch a bus, get away from this place of death. Nausea swept over her again but she shoved it away. She didn't have the energy to be sick.

'Mrs Eveldene?' The receptionist's voice made her pause.

'Yes?' It was so hard to make her voice work.

'You've dropped your cheque,' the girl said. She walked out from behind her desk, stooped to retrieve it and handed it to her. As she did, she checked it, and her eyes widened.

'Wow,' she said. 'You wouldn't want to lose this, would you?'

Matt stood outside the funeral parlour, dug his hands deep into his pockets and stood absolutely still, waiting for the waves of shock and grief to subside. The image of Jess was burned on his retinas. His beautiful, adored big brother. His Jess, wasted, cold and dead on a mortuary slab.

He felt sick to the core. The anger inside him was building and building, but he knew deep down that it was only a way to deflect grief.

If he let his anger take hold he'd walk right back in there, pick up that piece of flotsam and shake her till her teeth rattled, but it would do no good at all. For that was all she was, a piece of detritus picked up somewhere along Jessie's useless mess of a life.

What a sickening waste.

But suddenly he found himself thinking of the girl inside, of those huge, desperate eyes. Another life heading for nothing.

But those eyes…that flash of anger…

That was more than waste, he thought. There was something that Jess had loved, even a kind of beauty, and, underneath the anger, part of him could see it.

He could turn around and try and help.

Yeah, like he'd tried to help with Jess. Useless, useless, useless.

He'd given her money to survive. 'Don't waste it all,' he found himself saying out loud, to no one, to the girl inside, to the bright Hawaiian sun. But it was a forlorn hope, as his hopes for Jessie had always been forlorn.

Enough. It was time to move forward. It was time to forget the waif-like beauty of the girl inside this nightmare of a place. It was time to accompany his brother's body home for burial.

It was time to get on with the rest of his life.

CHAPTER ONE

SHE HAD THE best job in the world—except right now.

Dr Kelly Eveldene was the physician in charge of the International Surf Pro-Tour. For the last four years she'd been head of the medical team that travelled with the world's top surfers. She was competent, she was popular, she understood the lingo, and she knew so many of the oldtimer surfers that the job suited her exactly.

There were a couple of downsides. This year the pro tournament had moved to Australia for the world championships. She wasn't happy about coming to Australia, but Australia was big. The other Eveldenes lived in Sydney and the surf championship was to be held on the Gold Coast in Queensland. Her chances of running into…anybody were minuscule.

She'd done the research now. Henry Eveldene—her ex-father-in-law—was a business tycoon, rich beyond belief, and Eveldene was an uncommon name. Still, surely the presence in the country of a couple of inconspicuous people with similar names wouldn't come to his attention.

Her other quibble was that Jess was competing this year, his first time out of juniors. He was seventeen years old, surf mad and as skilled as his father before him. She couldn't hold him back and she didn't want to try. Her son was awesome. But now, at this level, with the surf so big and Jess trying so hard, she had qualms.

She had qualms right now.

She was in the judging tent on the headland, as she always was during competition. There were paramedics on jet skis close to the beach, ready for anything that happened in the surf. In the event of an accident she'd be on the beach in seconds, ready to take charge as soon as casualties were brought in. If it looked like a head or spinal injury—and after long experience with the surf she could pretty much tell from seeing the impact what to expect— she'd be out there with the paramedics, organising spinal boards from the jet ski, binding open wounds so they didn't bleed out in the water, even doing resuscitation if it was needed.

The job had its grim moments, but at this professional level she was seldom needed for high drama. What she dealt with mostly were cuts, bruises, rashes and sunburn, plus the chance to combine her medicine with the surfing she loved. It was a great job.

But now Jess was competing and her heart was in her mouth.

He had thirty minutes to show the judges what he could do. The first wave he'd caught had shown promise but had failed to deliver. It hadn't given him a chance to show his skills. He'd be marked down and he knew it. He hit the shallows, flagged down an official jet ski and was towed straight out again.

Then there was an interminable ten minutes when the swell refused to co-operate, when nothing happened, when he lay on his board in the sun while the clock ticked down, down. Then, finally, magically, a long, low swell built from the north-east, building fast, and Kelly saw her son's body tense in anticipation.

Please…

She should be impartial. She was an official, for heaven's sake.

But she wasn't impartial. She wasn't a judge. For this moment she wasn't even Dr Eveldene. She was Jessie's mother and nothing else mattered.

He'd caught it. The wave was building behind him, swelling with a force that promised a long, cresting ride. The perfect wave? He rode to the lip and crested down, swooped, spun, climbed high again.

But…but…

There was another wave cresting in from the south-east. The surfers called this type of wave a rogue, a swell that cut across the magic wave that had seemed perfect for the best of the rides.

Jess wouldn't be able to see it, Kelly thought in dismay, but maybe it wouldn't matter. Maybe his wave would peak and subside before it was interfered with. And even the waves crashed together, surely he'd done enough now to progress through to the next stage.

But then…

Someone else was on the rogue wave.

The surf had been cleared for the competition. No one had the right to cut across a competitor's wave. Only the competitors themselves were in the catching zone—everyone else was excluded. But a pod of enthusiastic juniors had set themselves up south of the exclusion zone, lying far out, hoping to get a better view of the surfer pros. This must be one of those kids, finding a huge swell behind him, unable to resist catching it, too much of a rookie—a grommet—to see that it would take him straight into a competition wave.

Uh-oh. Uh-oh, uh-oh, uh-oh.

The judges were on their feet. 'Swing off. Get off,' the judge beside Kelly roared. His voice went straight into the loudspeaker and out over the beach but the surfers were too far out, too intent on their waves...

Jess was in the green room, the perfect turquoise curve of water. He'd be flying, Kelly knew, awed that he'd caught such a perfect wave at such a time, intent on showing every ounce of skill he possessed. He'd be totally unaware that right behind...

No. Not right behind. The waves thumped into each other with a mighty crest of white foam. The grommet's surfboard flew as high as his leg rope allowed, straight up and then crashing down.

She couldn't see Jess. *She couldn't see Jess.*

That impact, at that speed...

'Kelly, go,' the judge beside her yelled, and she went, but not with professional speed. Faster.

This was no doctor heading out into the waves to see what two surfers had done to themselves.

This was Jessie's mother and she was terrified.

'Matt, you're needed in Emergency, stat. Leg fracture, limited, intermittent blood supply. If we're to save the leg we need to move fast.'

It was the end of a lazy Tuesday afternoon. Matt Eveldene, Gold Coast Central Hospital's orthopaedic surgeon, had had an extraordinarily slack day. The weather was fabulous, the sea was glistening and some of the best surfers in the world were surfing their hearts out three blocks from the hospital.

Matt had strolled across to the esplanade at lunchtime. He'd watched for a little while, admiring their skill but wondering how many of these youngsters were putting their futures at risk while they pushed themselves to their limits. No one else seemed to be thinking that. They were all just entranced with the surfers.

Even his patients seemed to have put their ills on hold

today. He'd done a full theatre list this morning, but almost
half his afternoon's outpatient list had cancelled. He'd been
considering going home early.

Not now. Beth, the admitting officer in Accident and
Emergency, didn't call him unless there was genuine need.
She met him as the lift opened.

'Two boys,' Beth told him, falling in beside him, walking fast, using this time to get him up to speed. 'They're
surfers who hit each other mid-ride. The youngest is a
local, fourteen years old, concussion and query broken
arm. It's the other I'm worrying about. Seventeen, American, part of the competition. Compound fracture of the
femoral shaft, and I suspect a compromised blood supply.
I've called Caroline—she's on her way.'

Caroline Isram was their vascular surgeon but Matt
knew she was still in Theatre.

'He'll need both your skills if we're going to save the
leg,' Beth said. 'Oh, and, Matt?'

'Yeah?'

'Coincidence or not? His surname's Eveldene.'

'Coincidence. I don't know any seventeen-year-old
surfer.'

Kelly was seated by the bed in Cubicle Five, holding Jess's
hand. It said a lot for how badly he was hurt that he let her.

He had enough painkillers on board to be making him
drowsy but he was still hurting. She was holding his hand
tightly, willing him to stay still. The colour of his leg was
waxing and waning. She'd done everything she could to
align his leg but the blood supply was compromised.

Dear God, let there be skilled surgeons in this hospital. Dear God, hurry.

'They say the orthopaedic surgeon's on his way,' she
whispered. 'The emergency doctor, Beth, says he's the

best in Australia. He'll set your leg and you'll be good as new.' *Please.*

'But I'll miss the championships,' Jess moaned, refusing to be comforted.

The championships were the least of their problems, Kelly thought grimly. There was a real risk he'd lose a lot more. Please, let this guy be good.

And then the curtains opened and her appalling day got even worse.

The last time Matt had seen his brother alive Jess had been in drug rehab. He'd looked thin, frightened and totally washed out.

The kid on the trolley when Matt hauled back the curtain was…Jess.

For a moment he couldn't move. He stared down at the bed and Jessie's eyes gazed back at him. The kid's damp hair, sun-bleached, blond and tangled, was spreadeagled on the pillow around him. His green eyes were wide with pain. His nose and his lips showed traces of white zinc, but the freckles underneath were all Jessie's.

It was all Matt could do not to buckle.

Ghosts didn't exist.

They must. This was Jessie.

'This is Mr Eveldene, our chief orthopaedic surgeon,' Beth was telling the kid brightly. The situation was urgent, they all knew it, but Beth was taking a moment to reassure and to settle the teenager. 'Matt, this is Jessie Eveldene. He has the same surname as yours, isn't that a coincidence? Jess is from Hawaii, part of the pro-surf circuit, and he's seventeen. And this is his mum, Kelly. Kelly's not your normal spectator mum. She was Jessie's treating doctor on the beach. She's established circulation, she's put the leg in a long leg splint and she's given initial pain relief.'

He was having trouble hearing. His head was reeling.

What were the odds of a kid called Jessie Eveldene turning up in his hospital? What were the odds such a kid would look like Jess?

Sure, this kid was a surfer and all surfers had similar characteristics. Bleached hair. Zinc on their faces. But... but...

The kid's green eyes were Jessie's eyes, and they were looking at him as Jess's had looked that last time.

Make the pain go away.

Focus on medicine, he told himself harshly. This wasn't his older brother. This was a kid with a compromised blood supply. He flipped the sheet over the leg cradle and it was all he could do not to wince. The undamaged foot was colourless. He touched the ankle, searching for a pulse. Intermittent. Dangerously weak.

'We took X-rays on the way in,' Beth told him. 'Comminuted fracture. That means there's more than one break across the leg,' she said, for Jessie's benefit. 'Matt, he needs your skill.'

He did. The leg was a mess. The compound fracture had been roughly splinted into position but he could see how it had shattered. Splinters of bone were protruding from the broken skin.

'Blood flow was compromised on impact,' Beth said softly. 'Luckily Jess has one awesome mum. It seems Kelly was on duty as surf doctor. She went out on a jet ski and got Jess's leg aligned almost before they reached the shore. The time completely without blood couldn't have been more than a few minutes.'

So it was possible he'd keep his leg. Thanks to this woman.

He glanced at her again.

Kelly?

It was impossible to reconcile this woman with the

Kelly he'd met so briefly all those years ago. This couldn't possibly be her.

But then her eyes met his. Behind her eyes he saw pain and distress, but also…a hint of steel.

Kelly. A woman he'd blamed…

'Well done,' he said briefly, because that was all he could think of to say. Then he turned back to the boy. If they had a chance of keeping this leg, he had to move fast. 'Beth, we need an ultrasound, right away. Tell Caroline this is priority. This blood flow seems fragile. Jess…' He had to force himself to say the name. 'Jess, you've made a dog's breakfast of this leg.'

'Dog's breakfast?' Jess queried cautiously.

'Dog's breakfast,' Matt repeated, and summoned a grin. 'Sorry, I forgot you were a foreigner.' Gruesome humour often helped when treating teens, and he needed it now. The anaesthetist needed Jess settled—and he needed to settle himself. 'It's slang. A working dog's breakfast is usually a mess of leftovers. That's what this looks like.'

'Ugh,' Jess said, and Matt firmed his grin.

'Exactly. We need to pin it back together and make sure enough blood gets through to your toes. That means surgery, straight away.'

The kid's sense of humour had been caught despite the pain. 'Cool…cool description,' he said bravely. 'Do you reckon someone could take a picture so I can put it on Facebook? My mates will think "dog's breakfast" is sick.'

'Sure,' Beth said easily. She'd stepped back to snap orders into her phone but she resurfaced to smile. Beth had teenage boys of her own. Priority one, Facebook. Priority two, fixing a leg. She waved her phone. 'I'll snap it now if that's okay with your mum. But then it's Theatre to make you beautiful again.'

'If your mother agrees,' Matt said.

Jess's mother. Kelly. Doctor in charge at the world surf championships.

Kelly Eveldene. The undernourished waif curled up in a funeral director's parlour eighteen years ago?

The images didn't mesh and Matt didn't have time to get his head around it. The boy's leg was dreadfully fractured, the blood supply had already been compromised and any minute a sliver of bone could compromise it again. Or shift and slice into an artery.

'You have my permission,' Kelly said, her voice not quite steady. 'If it's okay with you, Jessie?'

What kind of mother referred to her kid for such a decision? But Kelly really was deferring. She had hold of her son's hand, waiting for his decision.

Jessie. This was doing his head in.

Maybe he should pull away; haul in a colleague. Could he be impersonal?

Of course he could. He had to be. To refer to another surgeon would mean a two-hour transfer to Brisbane.

No. Once he was in Theatre this would be an intricate jigsaw of shattered bone and nothing else would matter. He could ignore personal confusion. He could be professional.

'Matt, Jessie's mother is Dr Kelly Eveldene,' Beth was saying. 'She's an emergency physician trained in Hawaii.'

'Mr Eveldene and I have met before,' the woman said, and Matt's world grew even more confused.

'So it's not a coincidence?' Beth said. 'Matt...'

Enough. Talking had to stop. History had to take a back seat. These toes were too cool.

'Jess, we need to get you to surgery now,' he told the boy. There was no way to sugar-coat this. 'Your leg's kinking at an angle that's threatening to cut off blood supply. Caroline Isram is our vascular surgeon and she's on her way. Together we have every chance of fixing this. Do we have your permission to operate? And your mother's?'

Finally, he turned to face her.

Kelly Eveldene had been a half-starved drug addict who'd been with his brother when he'd died. This was not Kelly Eveldene. This was a competent-looking woman, five feet six or seven tall, clear, grey eyes, clear skin, shiny chestnut curls caught back in a casual wispy knot, quality jeans, crisp white T-shirt and an official surf tour lanyard on a cord round her neck saying, 'Dr Kelly Eveldene. Pro Surf Medical Director.'

Mr Eveldene and I have met before.

'Are you a long-lost relative?' Jess asked, almost shyly. 'I mean, Eveldene's not that common a name.'

'I think I must be,' Matt said, purposely not meeting Kelly's eyes. 'But we can figure that out after the operation. If you agree to the procedure.'

'Dr Beth says you're good.'

'I'm good.' No place here for false modesty.

'And you'll fix my leg so I can keep surfing?'

Something wrenched in him at that. Suddenly he heard Jess, long ago, yelling at his father over the breakfast table. 'All I want to do is surf. Don't you understand?' And then saw Jessie arriving home from school that night, and finding his board in the backyard, hacked into a thousand pieces.

But now wasn't the time for remembering. Now wasn't the time to be even a fraction as judgmental as his father had been.

'I'll do my best,' he said, holding Jessie's gaze even though it felt like it was tearing him apart to do so. 'Jess, I won't lie to you—this is a really bad break, but if you let us operate now I think you'll have every chance of hanging ten or whatever you do for as long as you want.'

'Thank you,' Jess said simply, and squeezed his mother's hand. 'Go for it. But take a picture for Facebook first.'

* * *

She'd been a doctor now for nine years, but she'd never sat on this side of the theatre doors. She'd never known how hard the waiting would be. Her Jess was on the operating table, his future in the hands of one Matt Eveldene.

Kelly had trained in emergency medicine but surfing had been her childhood, so when she'd qualified, she'd returned. Her surfing friends were those who'd supported her when she'd needed them most, so it was natural that she be drawn back to their world. She'd seen enough wipeouts to know how much a doctor at the scene could help. Even before she'd qualified she'd been pushing to have a permanent doctor at the professional championships, and aiming for that position after qualification had seemed a natural fit.

But she'd spent time in hospitals in training, and she'd assisted time and time again when bad things had happened to surfers. She knew first-hand that doctors weren't miracle workers.

So now she was staring at the doors, willing them to open. It had been more than three hours. Surely soon…

How would Jess cope if he was left with residual weakness? Or with losing his leg entirely? It didn't bear thinking about. Surfing wasn't his whole life but it was enough. It'd break his heart.

And Matt Eveldene was operating. What bad fairy was responsible for him being orthopaedic surgeon at the very place Jess had had his accident? Wasn't he supposed to still be in Sydney with his appalling family? If she'd known he was here she would never have come.

Had she broken her promise by being here?

You keep yourself out of our lives, now and for ever.

She'd cashed the cheque and that had meant acceptance of his terms. The cheque had been Jessie's insurance, though. Her husband's insurance. Surely a promise couldn't negate that.

The cheque had saved her life. No, she thought savagely. Her Jess had saved her life. Her husband. Her lovely, sun-bleached surfer who'd picked her up when she'd been at rock bottom, who'd held her, who'd made her feel safe for the first time. Who'd had demons of his own but who'd faced them with courage and with honour.

'We'll get through this together, babe,' he'd told her. 'The crap hand you've been dealt…my black dog… We'll face them both down.'

But the black dog had been too big, too savage, and in the end she hadn't been able to love him enough to keep it at bay. The night he'd died…

Enough. Don't go there. In a few minutes she'd have to face his brother, and maybe she would have to go there again, but only briefly, only as long as it took to explain that she hadn't broken her promise deliberately. She and Jess would move out of his life as soon as possible, and they'd never return.

It took the combined skill of Matt Eveldene, a vascular surgeon, an anaesthetist and a team of four skilled nurses to save Jessie's leg.

'Whoever treated it on the beach knew what they were doing,' Caroline muttered. Gold Coast Central's vascular surgeon was in her late fifties, grim and dour at the best of times. Praise was not lightly given. 'This artery's been so badly damaged I have no idea how blood was getting through.'

She went back to doing what she was doing, arterial grafting, slow, meticulous work that meant all the differ-ence between the leg functioning again or not. Matt was working as her assistant right now, removing shattered slivers of bone, waiting until the blood supply was fully established before he moved in to restore the leg's strength and function.

If Caroline got it right, if he could managed to fuse the leg to give it the right length, if there'd not been too much tissue damage, then the kid might…

Not the kid. Jessie.

The thought did his head in.

'I think we're fine here,' Caroline growled. 'Decent colour. Decent pulse. He's all yours, Matt.'

But as Matt moved in to take control he knew it was no such thing.

This kid wasn't his at all.

The doors swung open and Matt Eveldene was in front of her. He looked professional, a surgeon in theatre scrubs, hauling down his mask, pushing his cap wearily from his thatch of thick, black hair. How did he have black hair when Jessie's had been almost blond? Kelly wondered absent-mindedly. He was bigger than Jess, too. Stronger boned, somehow…harsher, but she could still see the resemblance. As she could see the resemblance to her son.

This man was Jessie's uncle. Family?

No. Her family was her son. No one else in the world qualified.

'It went well,' he said curtly from the door, and she felt her blood rush away from her face. She'd half risen but now she sat again, hard. He looked at her for a moment and then came across to sit beside her. Doctor deciding to treat her as a mother? Okay, she thought. She could deal with this, and surely it was better than last time. Better than brother treating her as a drug-addicted whore.

The operation had gone well. She should ask more. She couldn't.

There was only silence.

There was no one else in the small theatre waiting room. Only this man and her.

There were so many emotions running rampant in her mind that she didn't have a clue what to do with them.

'Define...define "well",' she managed, and was inordinately proud of herself that she'd managed that.

'Caroline had to graft to repair the artery,' he told her. 'But she's happy with the result. We have steady pulse, normal flow. Then I've used a titanium rod. You know about intramedullary nailing? There wasn't enough bone structure left to repair any other way. But the breaks were above the knee and below the hip—well clear—so we've been able to use just the one rod and no plates. He has a couple of nasty gashes—well, you saw them. Because the bone fragments broke the skin we need to be extra-cautious about infection. Also Caroline's wary of clotting. He'll spend maybe a week in hospital until we're sure the blood flow stays steady. After that, rest and rehabilitation in a controlled environment where we know he can't do further damage. You know this'll be a long haul.'

'It'll break his heart,' Kelly whispered. 'It's going to be six months before he's back on a surfboard.'

'Six months is hardly a lifetime,' Matt said, maybe more harshly than he should have. 'He'll have some interesting scars but long term nothing a surfer won't brag about. Depending on his growth—at seventeen there may or may not be growth to come—we may need to organise an extension down the track but the rod itself can be extended. Unless he grows a foot he should be fine.'

So he'd still be able to surf. She hadn't realised quite how frightened she'd been. She felt her body sag. Matt made a move as if to put a hand on her shoulder—and then he pulled away.

He would have touched her if she'd been a normal parent, she thought. He would have offered comfort.

Not to her.

It didn't matter. He'd done what she'd most needed him to do and that was enough.

She made to rise, but his hand did come out then, did touch her shoulder, but it wasn't comfort he was giving. He was pressing her down. Insisting she stay.

'We need to talk,' he said. 'I believe I deserve an explanation.'

She stilled. Deserve. *Deserve*!

'In what universe could you possibly deserve anything from me?' she managed.

'Jessie has a son!'

'So?'

'So my brother has fathered a child. My parents are grandparents. Don't you think we deserved to know?'

'I'm remembering a conversation,' she snapped, and the lethargy and shock of the last few hours were suddenly on the back burner. Words thrown at her over eighteen years ago were still vividly remembered. 'How could I not remember? Make no contact with your parents. Do not write. Never tell your mother Jess and I were married. Keep myself out of your lives, now and for ever. You said there were a hundred reasons why I should never contact you. You didn't give me one exception.'

'If you'd told me you were pregnant—'

'As I recall,' she managed, and it hurt to get the words out, 'you didn't want to know one single thing about me. Everything about me repelled you—I could see it on your face.'

'You were a drug addict.'

She took a deep breath, fighting for control. 'Really?' she asked, managing to keep her voice steady. 'Is that right? A drug addict? You figured that out all by yourself. On what evidence?'

He paused, raking his long, surgeon's fingers through

his thatch of wavy, black hair. The gesture bought him some time and it made Kelly pause. Her anger faded, just a little.

The present flooded back. This man had saved her son's leg. Maybe she needed to cut him some slack.

But it seemed slack wasn't necessary. He'd gone past some personal boundary and was drawing back.

'No,' he said. 'I made…I made assumptions when Jess died. I know now that at least some of them were wrong.'

Her anger had faded to bitterness. 'You got the autopsy report, huh?'

'You need to realise the last time I saw Jessie alive he was in drug rehab.'

'That was years before he died.'

'He told you about it?'

'Jess was my husband,' she snapped. 'Of course he told me.'

'You were seventeen!'

'And needy. Jess was twenty-four and needy. We clung to each other.' She shook her head. 'Sorry, but I don't have to listen to this. You never wanted to know about me before, and you don't now. Thank you very much for saving my son's leg. I guess I'll see you over the next few days while he's in hospital but I'll steer clear as much as I can. I need to go back to our hotel and get Jess's things, but I want to see him first. Is he awake?'

'Give him a while. We put him pretty deeply under.' He raked his hair again, looking as if he was searching for something to say. Anything. And finally it came.

'You weren't on drugs?'

'You know,' she said, quite mildly, 'years ago I wanted to hit you. I was too exhausted to hit you then, too emotionally overwrought, too wrecked. Now I'm finding I want to hit you all over again. If it wasn't for what you've just done for Jess, I would.'

'You looked—'

'I looked like my husband had just died.' Her voice grew softer, dangerously so. 'I was seventeen. I was twelve weeks pregnant and I'd sat by Jess's bedside for twenty-four hours while he lost his fight to live. Then I'd sat in the waiting room at the funeral home, waiting for you, hour upon endless hour, because I thought that it'd be his father who'd come to get him and I didn't think a message to contact me would work. I couldn't risk missing him. And then you walked in instead, and I thought, yes, Matt's come in his father's stead and it'll be okay, because Jess had told me how much he loved you. All I asked was for what Jess wanted, but you walked all over me, as if I was a piece of pond scum. And now...now you're still telling me I looked like a drug addict?'

There was a long silence. She didn't know where to go with this. She'd bottled up these emotions for years and she'd never thought she'd get a chance to say them.

Somewhere in Sydney, in a family vault, lay Jess's ashes. She'd failed the only thing Jess had ever asked of her. She hadn't stood up to his family.

She should hate this man. Maybe she did, but he was looking shocked and sick, and she felt...she felt...

Like she couldn't afford to feel.

'I'll grab Jess's things and bring them back,' she said, deciding brisk and efficient was the way to go. 'It's only ten minutes' walk to the hotel. I should be back before he's properly awake. The rest of the surfers will be worried, too. There are a lot of people who love my Jess—practically family. Thank you for your help this afternoon, Matt Eveldene, but goodbye. I don't think there's single thing left that we need to talk about.'

There was. She knew there was. She walked down the hill from the hospital to the string of beachside hotels where most of the surfers were staying and she knew this wouldn't end here.

Why did Jess look so much like his father? Why had she called him Jess?

Why had she kept her husband's name?

'Because it was all I had of him,' she said out loud, and in truth she loved it that her son was called Jessie, she loved that he loved surfing, she loved that when she looked at him she could see his father.

But not if it meant…loss?

Her husband had told her about his family, his father in particular. 'He controls everything, Kelly. It's his way or no way. He loathed my surfing. He loathed everything that gave me pleasure, and when I got sick he labelled me a weakling. Depression? Snap out of it, he told me, over and over. Pull yourself together. I couldn't cope. That's why I hit the drugs that first time.'

She knew as much as she ever wanted to know about Jessie's father—but he'd also told her about his brother, Matt.

'He's the only good thing about my family, Kell. If anything ever happens to me, go to him. He'll help you.'

Well, he had helped her, Kelly thought grimly. She thought of the insurance cheque. It had been tossed at her in anger but she owed everything to it.

'So Jess might have been wrong about him being a nice guy, but he's had his uses,' she told herself. 'Now forget about him. You have enough to worry about without past history. For instance, the surf tour's moving on. You'll need to take leave. You'll need a place to stay, and you'll need to figure a way to stop Jess's heart from breaking when he learns that he's no longer part of the surf circuit.'

He felt like he'd been hit with a sledgehammer.

Matt walked up to the hospital rooftop, to the cafeteria

area that looked out over the ocean. He leant on the rail
overlooking the amazing view, trying to let the enormity
of what had just happened sink in.

Jessie had a son. Somehow, his brother wasn't dead.

Okay, that was a crazy thing to think but right now that
was how it seemed. He knew if he phoned his mother—
'You have a grandson. He's named Jess and he looks just
like our Jessie'—his mother would be on the next plane.
She'd broken her heart when Jess had died, and she'd never
got over it. Always a doormat to her bully of a husband,
she'd faded into silent misery. Matt worried about her,
but not enough to stay in Sydney, not enough to stay near
his father.

Should he tell his mother? He must. But if he told his
mother, his father would know, too. There was the rub.
Could you fight for custody of a seventeen-year-old boy?
No, Matt thought, but knowing his father, he'd try. Or,
worse, he'd let loose the anger he still carried toward his
older son and unleash it on Kelly and his grandson.

The thought of his father bullying Kelly…

As he'd bullied her…

He thought back to the appalling funeral parlour scene
and he felt ill.

He'd been a kid himself, a student. The call had come
late at night; Jess had had a fall and died. Yes, it seemed
to be suicide. His body was at a Hawaiian funeral home
and a woman calling herself his wife was making the ar-
rangements.

His father had exploded with grief and rage. 'Stupid,
idiotic, surfer hop-head. You needn't think I'm heading off
to that place to see him. You do it, boy. Go and get him,
bring him home so his mother can bury him and there's
an end to it.'

'They say he's married?'

'He's been off his head for years. If there's a marriage

get it annulled. We have more than enough evidence to say he was mentally incapable. And don't tell your mother. Just fix it.'

But Jess had never been mentally incapable. The depression that had dogged him since adolescence had been an illness, the same way cancer was an illness. Underneath the depression and, yes, the drugs when he'd been using, he'd still been Jess, the gentle, soft-spoken big brother Matt had loved.

He might have known he'd have married a woman of spirit.

But a seventeen-year-old?

He'd judged her back then because of her appearance and obvious desperation, but things were making horrible sense now.

All apart from the age. Surely seventeen was under-age for marriage in Hawaii? They'd have needed special permission.

Had they done it because Kelly had been pregnant?

These were questions Matt should have asked years ago, not now.

The questions had been there, though. He'd flown home with Jessie's body and the questions had rested unanswered in the back of his mind. The image of a girl curled in utter misery, of a cheque floating to the floor, of a desperation he'd done nothing to assuage, these images had stayed with him. The questions had nagged while he'd qualified as a doctor, while he'd got himself away from his domineering father, while he'd attempted his own marriage… While he'd come to terms with life, as Jessie never had. Just as Kelly had obviously come to terms with her life.

He remembered his relief when he'd found the cheque had been cashed. Now I don't need to feel guilty, he'd told himself. But the questions had stayed.

They had been answered now—almost. She'd used the cheque, but to what purpose?

To train herself in medicine?

To raise another surfer like Jess?

If his father found out… To have a grandson addicted to surfing…

Better not to tell him. Better to leave things as they were, just get this kid well and on his way.

But he looked so much like Jess…

So? He'd be in hospital for a week or so and then an outpatient for longer with rehab. He'd see him a lot. He had to get used to it.

And his mother?

Her image haunted him. In truth, her image had haunted him for years and now there was this new image juxtapositioned on the old.

Should the new image make the haunting go away?

A surf doctor. What sort of doctor was that?

What sort of woman was that?

A woman with spirit.

How could he know that?

He just…knew. There was that about her, an indefinable strength. A beauty that was far more than skin deep.

Beauty? He raked his hair again, thinking he wasn't making sense. He was too tired, too shocked to take it in. He needed to go home.

At the thought of his home he felt his tension ease. Home, the place he'd built with effort and with love. Home with his dogs and his books.

His house was the only place where he was at peace. His home mattered. He'd learned early and learned hard; people only complicated that peace.

He needed to go home now and put this woman and her son out of his head.

He needed to be alone.

CHAPTER TWO

THE SURF CHAMPIONSHIPS lasted for two more days and Kelly worked for both of them. There were gaps in the day when she could visit Jess, but she had to work for as long as she could. She needed the money.

The surfing community looked after its own, but there wasn't a lot they could do to help. They'd need to employ another doctor for the next round of the championships in New Zealand. As soon as Jess was well enough for Kelly to rejoin the tour, the position was hers again, but pro-surfing ran on the smell of a surf-waxed rag, and they couldn't afford to pay her for time off.

And she would not use the trust fund.

She needed to move from the hotel. One of the locals offered her a basic surfer's squat and she accepted with relief. She'd find a decent apartment when Jess was released from hospital but until then she'd live in her surf squat and focus on Jess's recovery.

From Jessie's charts and from information she drew from junior doctors, she could track Jessie's progress. There was therefore no need to talk to Matt Eveldene. The advantage of Matt being head of the orthopaedic ward was that where Matt went, students followed. She could always hear him coming so she could give Jess a quick hug and disappear.

'Here come the medical cavalry. It's time to make my-self scarce.'

'He looks at me funny,' Jess said sleepily on the second day, and she hugged him again, feeling defensive about leaving him.

'Surgeons are a law unto themselves,' she said. 'If he only looks at you funny, you're getting off lightly. These guys spend their days looking inside people, not practis-ing social skills.'

The surf tour moved on. She spent a couple of hours of her first free day moving into her dreary little apartment. Back at the hospital she found Jess awake and bored, so she spent an hour going over the results of the champion-ship he'd missed out on, talking future tactics, as if those tactics might be useful next week instead of in six months.

Finally he went to sleep. What to do now? She knew how long rehabilitation would take. She had weeks and weeks of wondering what to do.

Okay, do what came next. Lunch. She slipped out to find some—and Matt was at the nurses' station.

Was he waiting for her? It looked like it. His hands were deep in the pockets of his gorgeous suit, he was talking to a nurse but he was watching Jess's door. As soon as he saw her, he broke off the conversation.

'Sorry, Jan,' he said to the nurse, 'but I need to speak to Mrs Eveldene.'

'That's Dr Eveldene,' she said as he approached, be-cause her professional title suddenly seemed important. She needed a barrier between them, any barrier at all, and putting things on a professional level seemed the sensible way to achieve it. 'Do you need to discuss Jessie's treat-ment?'

'I want lunch,' he growled. 'There's a quiet place on the roof. We can buy sandwiches at the cafeteria. Come with me.'

'Say "please",' she said, weirdly belligerent, and he stared at her as if she was something from outer space.

But: 'Please,' he said at last, and she gave him a courteous nod. This man was in charge of her son's treatment. She did need to be…spoken to.

They bought their lunches, paid for separately at her insistence. He offered but she was brusque in her refusal. She followed him to a secluded corner of the rooftop, with chairs, tables and umbrellas for shade. She spent time unwrapping her sandwich—why was she so nervous?—but finally there was nothing left to do but face the conversation.

He spoke first, and it was nothing to do with her son's treatment. It was as if the words had to be dragged out of him.

'First, I need to apologise,' he said. As she frowned and made to speak, he held up his hands as if to ward off her words. 'Hear me out. Heaven knows, this needs to be said. Kelly, eighteen years ago I treated you as no human should ever treat another, especially, unforgivably, as you were my brother's wife. I accused you of all sorts of things that day. My only defence was that I was a kid myself. I was devastated by my brother's death but my assumptions about him—and about you—were not only cruel, they were wrong.'

'As in you assumed Jess was back using drugs,' she whispered. 'As you assumed I was the same. An addict.'

'I figured it out almost as soon as I got back to Australia,' he said, even more heavily. 'The autopsy results revealed not so much as an aspirin. I should have contacted you again, but by then I was back at university and it felt…' He shook his head. 'No. I don't know how it felt. I was stuck in a vortex of grief I didn't know how to deal with. Somehow it was easier to shove the autopsy results

away as wrong. Somehow it seemed easier to blame drugs
rather than—'

'Unhappiness?'

'Yes.'

'Jess was clinically depressed,' she said. 'You're a doctor. You know it's different. He wasn't just unhappy; he
was ill.'

'No antidepressants showed up either.'

'He wouldn't touch antidepressants,' she said, not sure
where this was going, not sure that she wanted to go with
him. 'He'd fallen into addiction once and it terrified him.
In all the time I knew him, he took nothing.'

'How long did you know him?'

She shouldn't say. She didn't owe this man an explanation, and her story hurt. But it was also Jessie's story. It
hadn't been told and maybe…maybe Jess would want his
brother to know.

'*Get in touch with Matt if anything happens to me,*' he'd
said to her, more than once. '*He'll look after you.*'

If anything happens to me… He'd obviously been thinking suicide. It still played in her mind, and it was still unbearable. So many questions… The questions surrounded
her, nightmares still.

But maybe she had to expose a little of that pain. Matt
was waiting for her to speak, and after all these years his
gaze was non-judgmental. He wanted to know.

Eighteen years ago he hadn't asked, and she'd hated
him. But then he'd been young and shocked and grieving,
she conceded, and shock could be forgiven.

Almost. There was still a part of her that was that cring-
ing seventeen-year-old, remembering this man's fury.

'I met Jess when I was sixteen,' she said, forcing herself to sound like the grown-up that she was. 'And I was
a mess. But not because of drugs. I was just…neglected.
My father was interested in surf and booze and nothing

else. My mother disappeared when I was four—at least, I think it was my mother; my father never seemed sure. It didn't matter. It was just the way things were. I was dragged up in the surfing community. There were good people who looked out for me, but they were itinerant and there were lots who weren't so good. But all of them came and went. I stayed.'

'It must have been a tough upbringing,' he said quietly, and she nodded.

'You could say that. And then, of course, I reached my teenage years. I matured late, thanks be, but finally at six-teen I became…female, instead of just a kid. Then things got harder. Unprotected and often homeless, camping as we often did, I became a target and my father was little use. I was a little wildcat, doing my best to defend myself, but it couldn't last. Then Jess arrived. He set up on the outskirts of the camp, seemingly intent on surfing and nothing else. I didn't think he'd even noticed us but there was an ugly scene one night when someone offered my father money. I remember someone grabbing me as if he owned me.'

'You were so alone.'

'I… Yes.'

'With no one?'

'No one who cared.'

'Kelly—'

'It was a long time ago,' she said, and she even smiled a little. 'You know, when you spoke then, you sounded just like Jess. Just as angry on my behalf. That night he appeared out of the dark, out of nowhere, and he was fu-rious. I hit out—and Jess moved in before the guy could retaliate. He just…took over.'

'Jess was always bringing home strays,' Matt said. His instinctive anger seemed to have settled and his tone gen-tled. *Strays.* The word drifted in her mind. She knew no offence had been meant and none had been taken, because that's exactly what she'd been. A stray. Living in temporary surf camps. Going to school when the surf camp had been close enough or when her father had been capable of taking her. Living hand to mouth, the only constant being the surf.

But then there'd been Jess.

'He was the best surfer,' she said, pain fading as she remembered the way he'd transformed her life. 'He'd only just arrived but everyone there respected him. He was also…large.' She eyed Matt's strongly built frame, his height—six three or so—his instinctive anger on her behalf—and she remembered Jess. For some reason it made her want to reach out and touch this man, comfort him, take away the pain behind his eyes.

She could do no such thing.

'He told me he hadn't seen his family for years,' she went on, trying to ignore the urge to comfort Matt. 'By the time you saw his body the depression had left its mark. He hadn't been eating for weeks. But imagine him as I first saw him. He lived and breathed surfing. He was beautiful. He was built like a tank. No one stood up to him—and yet he stood up for me.'

'You became his lover?'

There was a moment's pause. She really didn't want to go there, but she needed to tell it like it was. For Jessie's sake. He'd been her hero, not some low-life who'd picked up teenage girls.

'No,' she said at last. 'Believe it or not, I was sixteen and that was how Jess treated me. Dad and I were living in a rough beach shanty, but Dad left soon after Jess arrived, looking for better surf on the other side of the island. He came back every so often, but Jess built a lean-to on the side of our hut and we stayed put. Jess said it was to protect me and that's what he did. He surfed with me, but it wasn't all fun. He pushed me to go to school. I'd been going intermittently but Jess insisted I go every day. He gave me money for clothes. He stopped Dad…well, he kept me safe. He was my gorgeous big brother. But then the black dog got too much for him.'

'The depression.'

'He called it his black dog. He said that's what Winston Churchill called it and that's what it felt like. A great black dog, always shadowing him. He said it'd been shadowing him since he was a kid, something he was born with. He told me how his dad hated it, thought he was weak because of it. He told me about how'd he'd tried to escape with drugs when he was in his late teens, and what a mess that had been. I think that was a way of warning me, because drugs were everywhere in our scene. But Jess wouldn't touch them. Never again, he said, even near the end when the depression was so bad and I pleaded with him to get help. "They'll only give me pills," he said, "and I'm not going down that road again."'

'If I'd known…'

'Jess said you didn't want to know,' Kelly said gently. 'Jess said you and he were close, but after rehab… He knew that shocked you. After he got his life together and the surfing was helping, he said he sent you the airfare to come and have a holiday together during your university holidays, but you wouldn't come.'

Matt closed his eyes and she saw the pain wash over him. No. It was more than pain. Self-loathing.

'He'd come out of rehab and gone straight back to surfing,' Matt managed. 'I thought—'

'You know, surfing and drugs don't really mix,' she said gently. 'There are always the fringe dwellers, people like my dad who surf a bit but who love the sun-bleached lifestyle more than the skill itself. But to be a real surfer you're up at dawn, day after day. The sea demands absolute attention, absolute fitness. You need to work as Jess did—he did casual bricklaying to pay bills—but he surfed at dawn and then he was back at dusk to surf every night, falling into bed with every single part of him exhausted. Jess used the surf to drive away his demons and it mostly worked. He had no time for drugs. I swear he wasn't taking them. I swear.'

'I believe you,' Matt said heavily. 'Now. But back then... I'd just found out my brother had killed himself and, what's more, that he'd married a seventeen-year-old just before he'd died. What was I to think? And then...pregnant?'

'That was my fault,' she said evenly, but he shook his head.

'Seventeen was hardly old enough to consent.'

'In those last months Jess wasn't fit enough to think of age differences,' she said evenly. 'The depression was so bad he just...went away. Physically he left for a couple of weeks and when he returned to camp he looked gutted. I was terrified. He was limp, unable to make any decisions. He didn't want to surf. He didn't want to do anything. If I told you all he'd done for me... Well, I was so grateful, I loved him so much, and the state he was in, I was terrified. Anyway, I did everything, anything I could think of to pull him out of it, and in the end I just lay down and held him. I held him all I could, every way I could, and when he finally took me I was happy because I thought he was coming out of it. I thought...he must be.'

'Oh, Kelly...'

'And I'd bought condoms—of course I had—and we used them, but that first time, well, I had the experience of a newt and I guess I was doing the seducing and I didn't do it right and then I was pregnant.'

'You told him?'

'He guessed. And for a while that woke him up. We had this first morning when we knew... I'd woken up sick and he waited until I was better and we took the boards out beyond the surf break to watch the dawn. And we lay there talking about our baby like it might really exist, about this new life that was so exciting. Life for both of us had been crap but this new life…we planned for it. And Jess told me I'd be an awesome mother and he'd try, he'd really try. But that was the last time…'

Her voice trailed off. 'The last time. We came back to shore and Jess found my dad and forced him to sign consent. We married but the dog was back, and with such force that Jess couldn't fight it. He…he went away. I searched and searched but then the police came to find me. And the rest you know.'

The rest he knew?

The rest he guessed.

He'd left a pregnant kid, his brother's widow, to fend for herself.

He'd left her with money. At least he'd done that.

But that had been the least he could do, and it had been her money anyway.

He should have brought her home.

To what? He'd still been a medical student; he'd had no income himself. He'd been sent by his parents to bring his brother's body home, not his brother's widow. If he'd arrived back with Kelly…his father could have destroyed her.

She was twisting a curl round and round her finger. It was a nervous gesture, showing she was tense. He suddenly wanted to reach out and take her hand in his. Hold her still. Take away the pain he'd helped inflict.

He didn't. He couldn't.

'Don't beat up on yourself,' Kelly said gently. 'Matt, it was eighteen years ago. We've moved on.'

'How did you manage?'

'You left me a cheque, remember? I stood outside that day, staring at this obscene amount on a slip of paper, and

I wanted to rip it up. And then I thought, this wasn't my money, it was Jess's, and I was carrying his baby. And I kept thinking of what Jess said to me over and over—"Babe, you're awesome, you can do anything." I thought of the biggest, best way I could keep his baby safe. "Go back to school." Jess had said it and said it. So I got a room with some surfing friends close to the high school and I went back.'

'And had a baby.'

'I had to stop for six months when Jessie was born,' she told him. 'But friends helped me out. I got choosy and I got stronger. My home was where my friends were, and I've made some good friends. It wasn't the easiest existence but finally I qualified and we were safe. Then, just after I got my first job in ER, a kid was hurt in an appalling surf accident. The surf pro-tour was in town and the kid had been hit in the neck by a stray board. He was moving after the accident, but he'd fractured C3. The bones shifted as he was being moved and he died almost as he reached us. The pro-tour organisers were so appalled they decided to fund a full-time medic. Career-wise it was my best fit, so here we are.'

'And what about Jess? Doesn't he go to school?'

'When we're in Hawaii. Otherwise he studies online. He's okay.'

'Online? That cheque was enough for a home,' Matt said roughly. 'It was enough to set you up for life.'

'I told you,' she said, and her voice wasn't rough but it was as determined as Matt's. 'My home's where my friends are. Jess and I have never needed bricks and mortar. Besides, that money is for Jess. Yes, I used some of it to become a doctor but I'm paying it back. By the time Jess turns twenty-one, his father's fund will be intact. He'll have an inheritance.'

'But what sort of career? Once my parents know—'

'Why would I want your parents to know?' She met his gaze, strong, sure, defiant, and he wondered how to answer that.

If his parents knew…

For his mother it'd be the most amazing gift. But his father…

Matt considered his bully of a father, and faltered.

He looked across the table at this amazing woman, and he thought…he thought…

'Tell me about Jess's leg,' Kelly said.

And he thought, yes. Medicine, that was easiest. Retreat to what he knew.

'It's looking okay,' he said. 'The open wounds are healing. We want him on IV antibiotics for another few days. The risks of bone infection after a compound fracture are too great to do otherwise. Caroline's positive about the arterial graft. The physiotherapists are already working with him—you'll have seen that. We're thinking minimal weight bearing in a couple more days, and then a slow rehab. Another few days in hospital until Caroline's happy and then six weeks as an outpatient.'

'I'd like to take him back to Hawaii.'

'You know the dangers of blood clots and swelling. Caroline will concur. Six weeks minimum before he flies.'

She'd known it. It was just hard hearing it. She'd have to get a decent apartment and it'd cost a bomb. She bit her lip, trying to hide her emotions.

There were always glitches. From the time she'd been born she'd been faced with glitches. Everybody faced them, she told herself. It was just that some of her glitches were a bit more major than others.

'Kelly—'

'My name is Dr Eveldene,' she snapped, and then flinched. She had to be polite. 'Sorry. This is not your business. You fix Jess, I'll do the rest.'

'I'd like to help.'

'You already did,' she said brusquely. 'You helped save Jess's leg and more. Eighteen years ago you threw me a cheque. It took me through medical school and it gave Jess and me a life. That's enough. I don't need more from your family.'

'It was,' he said slowly, 'your money.'

'You gave it to me.'

'I threw it at you, yes, but whatever I said at the time it was legally yours. My father made out insurance policies the day we were born—he values his assets, does our father, and he insures them all. But the policy was in Jess's name, which meant once Jess was married it was legally yours. If Dad had imagined that Jess intended marriage he'd have changed the policy in an instant, but you can't change the policy after death. Jess's marriage meant you inherited.' He hesitated. 'Jess knew about the policy. He must have known...'

'That I'd be safe,' Kelly whispered. 'Maybe that was even why... Oh, Jess...' She closed her eyes but then she opened them, moving on with a Herculean effort. 'All that's in the past,' she said. 'I need to look forward. I need to figure what to do for Jess.'

'You're broke?' he asked, and she flinched.

'I have money if I'm desperate, but I don't want to use it.' And then she took a deep breath, recovered, and fixed her gaze on his. 'I told you. I used Jess's insurance to put me through medical school, to get us a future, but I used as little as possible and I treated it as a loan. That money's sitting there waiting for Jess to need it as I needed it.'

'When he finally realises he can't spend his life surfing?'

Whoa. Where had that come from? Shades of his father?

'What are you saying?'

'He can't surf all his life.'

'That's his business.'

She was on her feet, backing away. 'Matt, if I hear you slight my son's lifestyle to him then, medical need or not, he's out of here. Your brother told me your father cares about possessions and power, and that's all. When he was ill, I suggested he might go home and you know what he said? "My father's home is where his things are. Home is where he can gloat over what he's achieved." But home for Jess and me is where my friends are. Our friends and the sea. And that's what we need now. We don't need your money or your judgement, Matt Eveldene. Leave us alone.'

CHAPTER THREE

HE SPENT A day letting her words sink in.

He spent a day feeling like a king-sized rat.

He also spent a day being proud of her. That she'd pulled herself up from where she'd been... That she was repaying her legacy... That she had the strength to stand up to him...

He was deeply ashamed of himself, but he was awed by Kelly.

'Jess married some woman!'

He was talking to himself while he walked on the beach near his house. His home was on a headland north of the town, surrounded by bushland and ocean. It hadn't rained for weeks. The country was parched but the scent of the eucalypts and the salt of the sea were balm to any man's soul.

And right now he needed balm.

His two dogs were by his side. Bess was a black Labrador, teenage-silly, joyfully chasing gulls, racing in and out of the waves as she tore along the beach. Spike was a fox terrier, a battered little dog from the lost dogs' home, and he went where Matt did. Spike put up with Bess's company when Matt was at work but when he was at home Spike belonged solely to Matt.

Spike was a dog a man could talk to.

'But why's she letting the kid go down the same road as his father?' Matt asked, stooping to scratch an ear Spike was having trouble reaching. He'd hurt Kelly. He knew he had and he hated it, but still he worried. 'All he seems to know is surfing. The first couple of days he was in hospital there were kids clamouring to visit. Now the tour's moved on, he's watching hour upon hour of surf videos. That's all he does. He's as fixated as Jess was.'

But the kid *was* Jess. The duplication of his brother's name was doing his head in. The likeness was doing his head in.

Kelly was doing his head in.

He'd noted her change of address on Jessie's medical records and he was appalled. Yesterday she'd moved into some kind of apartment at the back of an ancient Queenslander, a big old house up an enormously steep hill from the hospital. On his 'accidental' drive-by he'd decided it looked like it could blow down at any minute. It looked a dump.

She was spending most of her days with her son, but Jess was either sleeping or watching videos or playing video games. What sort of life was that for her? She had a couple of months of the same in front of her.

Dreary months.

It wasn't his business. She'd said that clearly. Back away.

How could he back away?

But to get involved…

See, there was the problem. Kelly had been right when she'd said his family cared for things rather than people. He did, too, but not for his father's reasons. His father accumulated possessions and gloated over them. Matt simply valued his home.

When he'd been a kid, Matt's older brother had been the centre of his world, and he'd been forced to watch as he'd slowly disappeared into his tortured illness. In defence Matt, too, had disappeared, surrounding himself now with his medicine and his home—a real home as opposed to the mausoleum his parents occupied.

His home, though, was solitary. For many, home meant family but it didn't for Matt. One failed marriage had shown him that.

Jenny had been a year younger than him, a colleague, ambitious and clever, warm and fun. His father had been critical but his father was always critical. His mother had approved.

'She's lovely and she's loving, Matt. You make sure you love her right back.'

He'd thought he had. They'd married. They'd bought a beautiful apartment overlooking Sydney Harbour and brought in an interior designer with the brief: 'We want it to be warm. We want it to be a home.'

They'd filled the house with gorgeous furniture and hundreds of books. They'd had separate studies, separate careers, but every night they'd slept together and Matt had felt like he had it all.

When Jenny had pulled the plug he'd been stunned.

'Matt, you love me but it's like I'm your imitation fireplace,' she'd told him. 'For decoration only. I want to keep you warm, but you have your own form of central heating. You're self-contained. You don't need me. I've tried to fit in with your beautiful life but I can't. Now I've met a farmer from west of nowhere. I'm off to be a country doctor, and raise sheep and kids, and have a very messy life and be happy. Good luck, Matt. I'll always love you a little bit. I'm just sorry that you couldn't love me a lot.'

That had been six years ago. He still didn't fully understand but after this time he conceded that maybe Jenny had been right. He wasn't husband material.

He'd moved to Queensland. He'd built a house he was immensely proud of and his career had taken over the gap that Jenny had left until he couldn't quite see where she'd fitted.

His parents' marriage was a disaster. He'd lost his brother and then he'd lost Jenny. There was no need to go down that emotional roller-coaster again. He was obviously a loner—except right now he wasn't. He kept thinking of a kid called Jess.

And he kept thinking of a woman called Kelly. A woman who twisted her curls around her fingers when she was tense. A woman he wanted to touch…

No. That was a road he wasn't going down. He needed to focus on practicalities.

And the foremost practicality? She was living in a dump because of some noble idea of saving her son's inheritance.

So what to do? Offer to pay for somewhere better? He thought of Kelly, of the fire in her eyes, of the hundred reasons she had to hate him, and he knew she'd refuse.

What, then?

He turned to stare up the cliff at his house.

Invite them to stay?

His house had a self-contained apartment, built so his mother could visit now and in the future. Wheelchair access. A veranda overlooking the surf. Its own television and internet access. Everything a disabled kid needed.

What was he thinking? Did he want them here?

Even if he offered, Kelly would refuse.

But if she didn't…

If she didn't then a kid called Jessie would be living in his house. Six weeks of Jess/Jess. Jess, his big brother. Jess, his nephew.

His nephew. His family.

He had to offer.

But when Jenny had accused him of self-containment, she'd been right. He didn't want to feel…the way he was feeling about Jess. Then there was Kelly. She was a woman he couldn't look at without feeling racked with guilt.

And then there was the way he felt when she twisted her curls…

The situation was doing his head in. He walked and walked, and when his cell phone rang and Beth was on the line, saying there'd been a car crash and he was needed, he was almost grateful.

Work, dogs, home, he told himself. They were all that mattered.

Except something else mattered. Someone else. Two someones.

He just needed space to get his head around it.

The car accident had been avoidable, appalling and tragic. One kid had a fractured pelvis but was so drunk it'd be morning before Matt could operate safely. He immobilised his damaged joint but that was all he could do for now. One kid had broken ribs and lacerations to his face. The broken ribs weren't life-threatening. The plastic surgeons would need to take over with this one.

The final casualty—the boy Beth had called him for because his spine was shattered—died just as he arrived.

So in the end there was little for him to do. Matt headed for the door, skirting the cluster of shattered parents, thanking heaven counselling wasn't his role.

Then he paused.

It was nine o'clock. Visiting hours ended at eight. He might be able to drop in and check on Jess without Kelly being present. Without being surrounded by students.

He might be able to talk to Jess by himself.

Why would he want to?

Because… Because…

There was no because. He had no reason, but almost before he thought it, he was in the orthopaedic ward, greeting the nurse in charge, shaking his head as she rose to accompany him, heading down the corridor alone to Jessie's room.

The nurse looked interested and he knew this visit wouldn't go unreported. The hospital grapevine was notorious. Having a kid in here who looked like him *and* shared his name had sent the rumour mill flying.

So what? Rumours didn't affect him and it was normal to visit patients after hours. Even a kid who looked like his...son?

But he was his nephew. Kelly had told Jess who he was. She'd obviously not told him the bleakest parts of their history, though, because the kid always greeted him with friendly interest. It was as he found it intriguing to have an uncle.

Uncle. The idea unnerved him.

Jessie's door was slightly open. He knocked lightly, not enough to wake him if he was sleeping, and pushed it further.

Jess was asleep, but he wasn't alone. Kelly was sitting by the bed, and even by the dim nightlight she looked ill.

'Kelly?' He said her name before he could stop himself. She wanted to be called Dr Eveldene. He'd tried to remember it. But now... What was wrong?

'Kelly,' he repeated, heading for the bedside, looking down at Jess, expecting something dire.

But Jess was deeply asleep. He had a good colour and his breathing was deep and even. Matt flicked back the bedclothes at the end of the cradle and checked the lower leg, using the small torch he often used for evening rounds. Good circulation. No problem.

He glanced again at Kelly. Problem.

She was wearing jeans and a light windcheater. Her curls were hauled back in a ponytail. Her eyes were deeply shadowed, as if she hadn't slept.

A row of welts ran from her chin down her neck and underneath the cover of her windcheater.

The doctor in him went straight into diagnosis mode. Shingles?

He tried to look more closely but she put her hands up to cover her neck. Defensively.

'Yes?' she said, and it was a dismissal in itself. *Yes, what do you want, how soon can you get out of here?*

'What's wrong?'

'Why are you here?'

'Nightly ward round,' he said as if he always did an evening round. He often did, he conceded. Just not to patients who were recovering nicely.

'You don't come in at night.'

'I do when I'm needed.' He relented. 'Car accident. Alcohol. Stupid. There was a death. An eighteen-year-old. Fractured spine, and he died before I could get here. I thought...'

And she softened, just like that.

'Oh, Matt,' she said, her tone suddenly understanding. 'I do that, too. See a kid's death, hug another kid. After I had Jess, that's where I'd be after trauma. Hugging. Jess always knows when I've had a bad day when the hugs are too tight. But...'

'But I have no right to hug Jess?'

'You don't,' she said flatly, but then she relented again. 'Kids killing themselves is the hardest thing.'

'Yet you let him surf.'

There was a moment's silence and when she finally spoke he could hear in her voice that he'd gone over that line again. 'You want me to pack him in cotton wool?'

'I... No. But he should have something other than surfing.'

'Butt out, Matt,' she said ominously, and he should. But right now he was facing a woman with an obvious problem.

Even if her name hadn't been Kelly Eveldene, he couldn't walk away. There was something…

'You want to tell me what's wrong?'

'No,' she said, but he moved before she could react, caught her hands and dragged them down from her neck.

Down the left side of her throat were red weals, clumping in groups of three, some so large they were running into each other. The mass was expanding as it disappeared under her windcheater. Heaven knew what sort of a mess was under her clothes.

'What's this?' He ignored her jerk of protest and concentrating on the welts. It looked like shingles, and yet not. These were angry clumps rather than the mass of irregular swelling that shingles caused.

She looked so unwell…

'Kelly, what did this?' he said gently. 'Can I help?'

'No.'

'Now, that's dumb,' he told her. 'If it's shingles we need to get antivirals on board right away. The sooner it's treated, the shorter the period of discomfort.'

'I know that,' she snapped. 'But it's not shingles.'

'Then what?'

'Bed bugs,' she said, goaded. 'I was dumb. You'd think I'd suspect. Haven't I lived in enough rough places in my time?' She wrenched away from him in sudden anger but the anger seemed to be self-directed. 'Leave it. I'm treating my room. These'll fade.'

'These'll give you hell,' he said, looking at the dark pools around her eyes. 'Did you get any sleep last night?'

'No, I—'

'They must be driving you crazy. Come down to Pharmacy and I'll get you antihistamines. I'll also get you an anaesthetic cream to give you immediate relief.'

'I don't need—'

'You do need,' he told her, and without waiting for

agreement he took her hand and tugged her to her feet.
'Suffering's for those who have no choice and you have a
choice. Jessie's asleep. He doesn't need you to look after
him now, Kelly. You, however, do need to look after yourself.'

How long had it been since things were taken out of her
hands?

They hadn't been. Ever. She looked out for herself.
Apart from that one blessed time around her briefest of
marriages, she'd been alone.

Even when she'd been tiny, when she'd been sick she'd
coped herself, and she was coping now. She'd woken in
the small hours covered with bed-bug sores. She'd spent
hours trying to rid her dump of an apartment of the crea-
tures, knowing how hard it was to eradicate them from
ancient crevices. She should find another place to stay but
the thought of paying any more for accommodation when
Jess was still in hospital horrified her. The insurance was
Jessie's money, college money, and it had to stay intact.

But the thought of going back there tonight made her
feel nauseous. Or maybe she felt nauseous because she'd
had so many bites. All she knew was that Matt Eveldene
suddenly had her by the hand and was tugging her through
the hospital toward his goal, the pharmacy. So, on top of
nauseous, she felt helpless as well.

She wasn't stupid. She'd taken an antihistamine that
morning. She managed to tell him.

'What strength? Do you have them in your purse? Show
me.'

'Matt, I'm a doctor.'

'Show me,' he growled again, and it was too much trouble to argue. She just did.

'You took one of these this morning?' He looked at the
packet with contempt. 'One?'

'I had stuff to do. I couldn't afford to be sleepy.'

'Yeah, you might go to sleep. What a disaster. This stuff won't even touch the sides. You can take much stronger medicine now, and stronger still when you're home in bed. But not in that bed.'

'I've sprayed.'

'It's a dump.'

'What business is that of yours?'

'You're my sister-in-law,' he growled. 'Family.'

'You are not my family!'

'Try telling that to every member of staff in this hospital.' She had to shut up then, while he threw orders to the woman in charge of Pharmacy. But even as he did, Kelly had to concede that he was right. She'd been aware of sideways glances and there'd even been straight-out questions. Now the pharmacist was filling Matt's scripts but she was looking from Matt to Kelly and back again, as if she could see family ties in the flesh.

Family? No way. She wasn't about to play happy families with an arrogant surgeon.

'Thank you,' she said stiffly, as the pharmacist handed over pills and cream. 'I'll pay—'

'I'm paying,' Matt snapped. 'And we need to get some of that cream on fast. I'll take you down to Emergency and we'll find a cubicle…'

'To do what?'

'Those welts are on your back. You can't reach them.'

'You're not putting cream on my back!'

'Don't be ridiculous. I'm a doctor.'

The pharmacist was watching them with interest, clearly enjoying herself. Clearly enjoying the sparks flying.

'I'll manage,' Kelly said stiffly.

'That's pig-headed.'

'You're not touching me.' She took the pills and cream from Matt's hands and backed out the pharmacy door. Matt followed, and she forced herself to stay still, to wait until the pharmacy door closed. She wanted to head straight for the exit but she had to be polite. This guy was Jessie's surgeon and he'd helped her. There was no need for her hackles to rise.

'Sorry,' she managed as the door closed behind them. 'I'm...I'm a bit of a private person.'

'How are you going to get that cream on your back?'

'I've been putting sunburn cream on my back for years. I'm a surfer, remember?'

He remembered. She could see it in the way his face closed down. And from the past...

'My family hates my surfing.' She could still hear Jess, her Jess, whispering to her all those years ago when he'd been in the throes of blackness. *'Don't they understand? When I'm surfing, I'm free.'*

She'd studied depression now; of course she had. When she'd first met Jess she'd had no clue, but she had enough knowledge now to know that he'd been treated the wrong way. Depression was an illness. If his surfing had been time out it should have been encouraged, not rejected. If he'd been encouraged to surf when he'd been a teenager, he might be alive now.

And now...

'Don't you dare judge,' she snapped, and Matt blinked and took a step back.

'I'm not judging.'

'Yes, you are. I can see it in your eyes. Surfing's a waste of space for you and your family.'

'It's a great sport,' he shot back. 'I surf myself. But you can't spend your life surfing.'

'You can if it's the only option,' she snapped. 'If your parents hadn't been so blind they'd have seen...they could have a kid who surfed or no kid at all. They gambled with their son's life and they lost.'

'Is that why you're letting Jessie surf?'

'You think that's why anyone wants to surf? Because they're ill? Butt out.'

'Kelly…'

'You know nothing.'

'I know plenty.' He raked his hair.

And she thought suddenly, he looks tired. Stressed.

Of course he did. He'd coped with road trauma to-night—a dead kid, grieving parents. And now she was laying ancient history at his door.

It wasn't his fault Jess had died. He'd been younger than Jess. The damage had been done by others, not by him.

'Kelly, I want you to come and stay with me,' he said, and her thoughts cut off dead right there.

Stay. With him?

'No.' It was an instinctive rejection; a gut reaction.

'Why not?'

'Because you're Jessie's doctor, nothing more. Because my problems are nothing to do with you.'

'We both know that's not true,' he said wearily. 'Kelly, my big brother loved you. I loved him. I wasn't there for you eighteen years ago and I should have been. There's not much I can do for you now, but I do have a large house with an invalid-friendly self-contained guest apartment. My mother comes to stay sometimes but it's free now. My housekeeper keeps the kitchen stocked and I have two dogs who need walks and company. There's a spare Jeep you can use, as long as you're comfortable driving on the left side of the road. It's a straight ten-minute drive to the hospital. I'm out most of the day. We'd hardly see each other. And best of all, last time I looked I didn't have a single bed bug.'

'No,' she said again, but she didn't sound as sure. She didn't feel as sure.

It was a great offer. Why say no?

Instinct, she thought. Pure animal instinct. There was something about this man that seemed...dangerous.

'Besides,' he said gently, 'I'd really like the opportunity to get to know your Jessie. I'm his uncle. I know he's had no one in the past...'

'He's had me. He's had the surfing community.'

'Don't you think he should be given the chance to have more?'

'Not if it messes with his head,' she said bluntly. 'Not if it means one trace of judgement.'

'There won't be judgement.'

'There already is. You're judging me for letting him surf.'

'I won't judge him.'

'No,' she said again, but she was faltering.

Her son was an Eveldene. Her son was this man's nephew.

Somewhere there was a bully of a grandfather, a man she never wanted to meet, but Jess had loved Matt—and his mother.

Her son had a grandmother, too.

Family was such an alien concept. She'd never had so much as a cousin.

Actually, probably she had. It was just that by the time she'd been old enough to know them her father had driven them away.

As Matt's father had driven his son away?

My mother comes to stay sometimes. That's what he'd said. Nothing about a father there.

But maybe there were similarities between Matt and his father. There were definitely similarities between Matt and his brother. Maybe that was why she was looking at him now and feeling...feeling...

She didn't know how she was feeling.

Matt looked like her husband, like her son. Maybe that

was it—but she knew it wasn't. It was the way he looked at her, as if he was as confused as she was. As vulnerable?

That was a nonsense. He was a chief orthopaedic surgeon, successful, gorgeous and at the top of his game. Vulnerable? Ha!

And he really was gorgeous. Long, lean and ripped. He looked…

Um, no. This wasn't what she should be thinking right now. Or thinking ever. Move on, she told herself. The hormonal rush she was feeling must be her emotions flaring up at his similarities to her long-dead husband, surely. Surely it had nothing to do with Matt.

Concentrate. She'd just been thrown an offer. If she accepted she wouldn't have to go back to her dump of an apartment tonight.

She shouldn't be so pig stubborn about the trust money, she told herself, not for the first time, but there was still the remembrance of that cheque, thrown at her in anger. Her initial urge to rip it in half was still with her. Only the thought of the baby inside her had stopped her. And now… She didn't want to use Eveldene money. She didn't want Eveldene hospitality.

She was also just a little bit scared of how this man made her feel.

'Come home,' Matt said, quite gently, and she realised he'd been waiting patiently for her to come to a decision.

'Home is where Jess is,' she said, too fast, and he grinned.

'There's not a lot of room in his hospital bed,' he said. 'You sound like you've had a lot of temporary homes. What's wrong with making one of them with me?'

'Matt…'

'I know, every part of me repels you,' he said ruefully. 'And I understand that. But for now, what I'm offering is sensible. Let's go find an all-night supermarket and buy you what you need.'

'I can collect my stuff.'

'It'll have to be fumigated before we transfer it.'

'How do you know?'

'I'm a dog owner,' he said. 'I'm used to fumigating.'

'You want to fumigate me?'

'A shower and a washing machine might do the job.'

A shower and a washing machine...

Of all the seductive things Matt could have said to her, that was the one most likely to succeed. A shower and a washing machine...

She knew her gear would be infected by bed bugs. She'd thought of doing a massive laundromat clean today but the thought of taking bedding by taxi had seemed too hard. She'd wanted to be with Jess, and she'd felt ill.

'You have a washing machine?' she said weakly.

'A really big one,' he said, like it was a siren lure, and it was. He smiled and his smile was suddenly tender, as if he'd realised she'd reached the end of her protests. 'Entice-ment by washing machine,' he said, echoing her thoughts. 'Come home with me, Kelly Eveldene, and see your wash-ing go round and round and round.' He reached out and touched her then, tracing a long, strong finger down her cheekbone. It was a feather-light touch, a touch that meant nothing, but for some reason it made her want to sink against him. Dissolve...

'Give in, Kelly,' he said softly. 'I'm not threatening your independence. I'm not threatening anything. But I am of-fering you respite, a clean bed and a machine with six wash cycles. Let me take you home.'

And what was a girl to say to that? She looked up at him and tried to speak but for some reason she was close to tears and she couldn't.

It didn't matter. Matt took her shoulders and turned her round and steered her out the back to the hospital car park.

And took her home.

CHAPTER FOUR

THE LAST TIME Kelly Eveldene had felt completely out of control had been the night she'd had Jess. She felt out of control again now.

She was sitting in Matt Eveldene's gorgeous Aston Martin, heading out of town towards who knew where? On the back seat was a parcel of stuff bought at the late-night supermarket, an oversized T-shirt and knickers, toothbrush, toothpaste, a hairbrush. In the trunk was her duffel bag, carefully sealed in two layers of plastic.

The antihistamine was kicking in. She didn't feel quite as itchy but she felt…dirty.

She still wanted to scratch but she wasn't going to scratch in this man's car. Imagine if she dropped a bed-bug egg into the leather?

'If you scratch, you risk infection,' he said, and she glanced across and realised he'd been watching her hands clench and unclench on her lap.

'I won't scratch,' she muttered.

'Good girl.'

'I don't think an Aston Martin with bed bugs would suit your image.'

'I'm thinking you'll have showered this morning and given those clothes a good shake before you put them on. My risk is minimal.'

'Yet still you took it,' she muttered. 'Jess always said you were hero material.'

'Did he?' he said, and she saw his hands grip hard on the steering-wheel.

'He said you stood up to your father.' She might as well say it. It took her mind off the itching—or some of it.

'Jess couldn't,' Matt said grimly. 'Or rather when he tried it didn't work. It wasn't that I was a hero. It was just that when Dad hit me I refused to fall over. I figured from the time I was tiny that showing hurt made me more vulnerable. I just…dissociated myself. Jess, on the other hand, didn't have it in him to dissociate himself. Every punch, it was like it was killing him inside.'

'Your father punched?'

'Yes,' he said curtly.

'Do you still see him?'

'Seldom.'

'But you still see your mother?'

'When Dad's overseas. But she's never had the courage to leave him. I sometimes think she would have, but after Jess died any shred of self-worth she had died with him. She's just…shrivelled. Dad doesn't hit her. He hasn't needed to. Sometimes I think there are worse ways of controlling than physical violence.'

'And that's why Jess…'

'Got sick? Who knows with mental illness? But if I had to take a punt I'd say it certainly didn't help matters. And I hardly supported him either.' There was anger behind his words, impotent fury, and his knuckles on the steering-wheel showed white. But then he seemed to make an effort to recover, forcibly relaxing his hold, forcibly relaxing the muscles around his mouth. 'Sorry. Ancient history.'

'You blame yourself? You were four years younger. But your father—'

'I said it was ancient history,' he snapped again.

'If your mother's still with him then it's current affairs.'

'Current affairs I can't do anything about. Except protect you from him.'

'Why would I need protecting?'

'You might,' he said grimly, 'if he knew he had a grandson...'

'You won't tell him?'

'No.'

'Thank you,' she said in a small voice. She was feeling more and more out of control.

They were heading into what looked like dense bushland. Where was he taking her?

The car swung off the main road onto what looked like a private driveway, but this was no manicured garden. It was still bushland but solar lights nestled among the trees on either side of the track, some glowing brightly, some just faint traces of light, depending, she guessed, on how much sun they'd received during the day. The effect was strangely beautiful.

Isolated and beautiful.

She was heading into nowhere with a man called Matt Eveldene. If she had been back in her surfing days all her senses would be telling her to get out of the car now. But she wasn't a kid and she was no longer defenceless—she hoped.

But still...

'You're quite safe,' he said, guessing her thoughts, and she flushed.

'I never thought...'

'You'd have been foolish not to have thought. This looks like the end of the earth, but in the morning you'll wake up and look over the ocean and you'll almost see Hawaii. Almost home.'

Almost home.

Home... There was a word to give her pause.

A home was what Jess needed now, for a while. But apart from their shoebox studio apartment back in Hawaii, where was home?

Home was work. Home was childcare when Jess had been little, school, university, libraries where she'd studied, with Jess reading or drawing pictures beside her, public playgrounds, beaches, friends' houses. Home was the surf, dawn and dusk. Home was where Jess was.

'Hawaii's hardly home any more,' she said, thinking aloud.

'Where is it, then?'

'Wherever Jess is. Wherever the surf is.'

'No roots?'

'I don't believe in them,' she said, and then for some reason she continued, revealing stuff she didn't normally reveal. 'As a kid I had a stuffed rabbit. Wherever Bugs was, that was home. Then when I was about eight one of my Dad's mates used Bugs to stoke a campfire. Home's never been anywhere since.'

'Hell, Kelly...' And there it was, that retrospective anger on her behalf. Jessie had reacted to stories of her past with fury. But who'd been angry on her behalf since?

No one. But it didn't matter, she told herself. And this man's concern shouldn't make her feel... She wasn't sure how she was feeling.

Push past it, she told herself. She didn't need this man feeling sorry for her. She didn't need this man looking at her with concern.

'It's no use worrying about what's in the past,' she managed. 'And what good did your fancy home do you or Jess? You need people. You don't need homes.' She meant it, too—but then they rounded the last bend in the driveway.

'This is home,' Matt said in a voice she hadn't heard before. 'I'm thinking this home almost equates to Bugs.'

Maybe it did. Sort of.

The house was long and low, nestled into the surrounding bushland almost as if it was part of it. It was built of sand-coloured stone, with wide verandas and a low-pitched roof, with tiny solar lights all around the veranda. Two dogs stood on the top step like two sentinels. A couple of battered surfboards leaned on the rail and a kayak lay near the steps. It looked like the perfect seaside homestead. It was picture-postcard perfect, though in postcards the dogs might have matched. These two were polar opposite, one a boof-headed Labrador, one a pint-sized fox terrier.

The dogs stood perfectly still until the car came to a halt, and then they whirled down the steps like a fire-cracker had exploded behind them. They raced round and round the car like crazy things until Matt opened his car door. The Labrador kept on whirling but the little dog timed it perfectly. Her circuit ended in a flying leap, straight onto Matt's knee. She gave an adoring yip, and then ceased all movement and gazed enquiringly at Kelly.

She had to laugh. What the little dog meant couldn't have been plainer if she'd been able to speak.

Matt, I'm really, really pleased to see you, but who is this? I need an introduction before we proceed.

'Spike, this is Dr Eveldene,' Matt said gravely, and to Kelly's delight Spike raised a paw and waited, just as gravely, for it to be shaken.

'Call me Kelly,' Kelly said, and Matt grinned.

'Does that go for me, too?'

'I…' She sighed. 'Of course. Sorry.' And then she couldn't say anything else because the Labrador was now in the car, welcoming them both home with far less re-finement and far more exuberance than Spike had shown.

Matt grabbed her gear. He dumped her plastic-shrouded duffel bag on the veranda—'That'll wait until morning'—then escorted her, with Spike leading the way, to his guest quarters.

He opened the door, flicked on the lights and she gasped in delight.

It was a self-contained apartment, furnished simply but beautifully. Polished wooden floors were softened with Persian rugs. The furniture looked comfortable and even a little faded, as if the curtains were left wide every day and the sun was left to do its worst. There were two bedrooms leading off the small sitting room. Matt led the way into the first, and flung open wide French windows while Kelly looked longingly at the truly sumptuous bed.

'All this for your mother?'

'Friends come here from Sydney, too,' he said briefly. 'I like them to be self-contained and I like my independence. You'll need to have breakfast with me tomorrow because I didn't think to get supplies, but from then on you can do your own thing. Leave the windows wide for a while—it's a bit musty in here. Would you like a drink? Anything?'

But she was still looking longingly at the bed, and through the door to the bathroom. A long, cool shower to get the heat out of the bites...

'Make sure the water's no hotter than body temperature or you'll make it worse,' Matt said, following her gaze. He dumped her stuff on a luggage stand and put the pharmacy items on the dresser. 'Are you sure you can put this cream on after your shower?'

'I... Yes.'

'I'll leave you to it, then,' he said. 'Goodnight, Kelly. Come on, guys, let's leave the lady to sleep.'

And he clicked his fingers and he was gone. The dogs went with him and he closed the door behind him.

Good. Excellent. She had all the privacy a girl could ask for.

Shower. Bed.

Home?

She didn't do home; she never had. To invest in a permanent base would have meant spending all the money she'd had, and it had seemed wrong. The money had never seemed hers. It was her son's, and it would stay intact for him.

So she'd rented places that would do. On the surf circuit, as part of her job, they'd stayed in decent hotels, but nowhere as good as this.

This was pure comfort. She could sink into bed right now, if she didn't feel so dirty.

She flicked off the lights, stripped naked and tossed her clothes out onto the veranda. She'd cope with them in the morning. Then she headed for the shower. No tiny bedbug egg was going to get into this place—it'd be a travesty.

Still, there was a niggle. Matt had given her this. She'd be beholden to him, and she didn't want to be any more beholden than she already was.

But... 'I don't owe Matt,' she told herself. 'The insurance was Jessie's. He's done nothing for me but hand me what was rightfully mine.'

He'd saved her son's leg. She'd studied the X-rays. She'd even—heaven forgive her for her lack of trust—scanned them and sent them to a guy she'd trained with who'd gone on to specialise in orthopaedics in the US. The response had come back, loud and clear.

'These before-and-after X-rays are truly impressive, Kelly. That's one hell of a break. Whoever did the repair has saved Jess a lifetime of limping.'

So, yes, she was grateful and here she was, in his home. She was in his bathroom, to be precise, because she'd wasted less than ten seconds getting from naked to under the water.

Matt was right through the wall. Jess's brother.

Was that what was doing her head in? The similarity between Matt and her husband?

It must be, she thought. There was no other explanation, because she was feeling…strange.

Out of control?

It was the bed bugs, she told herself, and the weariness, and the shock of the last few days. Even so, sitting by Matt in the car, following him as he'd strode through the supermarket, figuring out what she needed, knowing that he was…caring…

He didn't care. He was simply doing the right thing for once.

But the concept of caring was insidious. If he did…

He did. He'd been angry on her behalf. And he'd looked at her in such a way…

'Oh, stop it,' she told herself, lathering her hair for the second time with the gorgeous shampoo provided. She must have soap in her eyes. She was getting teary, and she didn't get teary. For some reason the thought of someone caring was almost overwhelming in its sweetness.

She coped alone. She'd always coped and she'd cope again. But for now…for now it was enough to stand under Matt's wonderful shower and then fall into Matt's wonderful bed…

Um…

Another image. Not a wise one. A totally stupid one, in fact. One started by his concern and moving to something else.

Matt was Jessie's brother. You did *not* have fantasies about your husband's brother.

Jess had been dead for eighteen years.

There'd been the occasional fling since—of course there had. Kelly was no black-clad widow, mourning her husband for ever. In fact, sometimes it seemed to her that Jess had been less her husband and more a wonderful, loving friend, someone who'd taken her out of a bad place but who'd been in a dreadful place himself. They'd been two kids fighting demons and Jess had lost.

She'd mourned him but she'd got on with her life, and occasionally a guy had turned up in her orbit. Never seriously, though. She was too busy, too preoccupied, not interested enough.

But Matt...

'Stop it,' she said out loud, and lathered her hair for a third time for good measure. 'Of all the times to indulge in fantasies... Inappropriate, inappropriate, inappropriate. Get yourself dry and into bed.

'Yes, Doctor,' she told herself, and managed a grin. Ooh, that bed...

As if on cue, one of the bites on her back stabbed with pain. Ouch. She turned the water colder and winced.

She had Matt's cream. Dry yourself off and get it on, she told herself. Bed's waiting.

Matt took the dogs for a fast walk out to the headland and then headed back to the house. For some reason he needed to be near. He'd told Kelly she could be independent but...but...

It didn't quite work. He'd like to be making her supper, making sure her bites were coated, making sure she was safely in bed.

Bed. His mind went all by itself to the memory of Kelly looking longingly at the bed.

A bed built for more than one.

Was he out of his mind? He was not interested in her like that. Not!

She was Jessie's wife. If he thought of her as his sister-in-law...

Logically it should help.

It didn't.

He headed back up the veranda and saw her open windows. Her clothes were heaped outside. He grinned. Very wise. He gathered them gingerly and took them to the laundry where he'd dumped her duffel bag.

Did bedbugs escape from laundries?

On impulse he tossed the clothes into the washing machine then unzipped her bag. Clothes only, he told himself; he wasn't looking at anything else.

He could do this. Confirmed bachelors—or confirmed divorcés—were good at laundry.

Most of her stuff was coloured. It all went into the machine. Her delicates—cute delicates, he noticed, before admonishing himself once again—went into the tub to soak. Then he found a can of insecticide, sprayed the room to within an inch of its life and carefully closed all the doors. No sucker would get out of there alive.

Job done. He should go to bed himself. He had an early start in the morning.

Instead, he found himself out on the veranda again, glancing along, seeing Kelly's windows were still open.

Her light was still on.

Why? She was dead on her feet. She should be in bed by now.

When she went to bed was her business—or maybe she slept with the light on.

Maybe there were shadows in her past that demanded nightlights.

Yeah, that didn't bear thinking of. Her past didn't bear thinking of. Thank God Jess had been able to help her.

And suddenly something lightened just a little inside him. His grief for his older brother had stayed raw, even after all this time. What a waste. The mantra had played over and over in his head—the thought that because his father had rejected his illness, Jess had died alone. Jess had had no one.

But he hadn't died alone. He'd had Kelly. She'd held him

and loved him and she'd told him she was bearing his child. And Jess had known of the insurance. No matter how ill he'd been, Jess would have known Kelly would be provided for. He'd have known she and her child would be safe.

And in that moment the gaping bleakness of Jessie's loss lessened, faded. It shifted to a corner of his mind where he knew it could stay in peace for the rest of his life. What a gift! And Kelly, this slip of a girl who'd turned into a woman of such strength, had given it to him.

Kelly, whose light was still on. Because of demons? Because…?

He heard himself call out before he knew he intended to. 'Kelly? Are you all right? Is there anything you need?'

There was a moment's silence. The dogs by his side seemed to prick up their ears, as if they, too, were listening for a response. And finally…

'I'm not as clever as I thought,' she said, sounding exasperated. She was just through the window.

'You want to expand on that?' he asked cautiously.

'Fine,' she said, goaded. 'I've always been able to put sunburn cream on myself. All over. But some time over the last few years, being with Jess rather than alone, I must have lost the knack. "Do my back," I'll say, and Jess does. There are bites on my back that are driving me nuts and I can't reach them.'

'You want help?'

There was a moment's silence. Then: 'I've only got a T-shirt and knickers on.'

'And if I'm to help you'll need to get rid of the T-shirt. Kelly, I'm a doctor.'

'Yes, but—'

'I'll do it with my eyes closed,' he told her, and she snorted.

'Right.'

'You want help or not?'

Another silence. Another moment's hesitation. Then, finally, the French windows were thrust wider and Kelly appeared in the light.

This was a Kelly he hadn't seen before. Her curls were damp and tangled. She was wearing her oversized man's T-shirt. Underneath she'd be wearing the cheap knickers the supermarket stocked, but that was all.

The T-shirt material was cheap and thin. A bit too thin. The shower had been cold...

'You said you wouldn't look,' she said coldly, and he shut his eyes.

More silence.

'Matt?'

'Yes?' he said cautiously. She was sounding...even more goaded.

'I'm a patient,' she said. 'I'm going to lie face down on the bed and pull up the T-shirt and you're required to apply medication.'

'It'd be better if you took the T-shirt off altogether.'

'Better for who?'

'I'm a doctor,' he reassured her. 'And you know I'm right. The night's warm. You're better sleeping with nothing on at all.'

'I might,' she conceded. 'After you leave.'

'After the doctor has done what he needs to do,' he agreed. 'Kelly...'

'Yes?'

'Go lie on the bed and we'll get this over with.'

She stripped off her T-shirt with her back to him—asking him to leave the room again would have seemed... prissy. Then she lay face down on the crisp, clean sheets and waited for him to do his worst.

His best? Surely his best. She needed help. All he had to do was take the cream from the bedside table and rub it in.

She heard him lift the tube, imagined him squeezing the cream onto those gorgeous surgeon's hands...

What was she doing, thinking of those hands?

She was actually thinking of more than his hands.

You're a sad case, Kelly, she told herself. One good-looking guy wanders into your orbit and your body reacts like...

Her body certainly did react. The moment his fingers touched her skin, she felt every sense respond. It was like her body lit up from within, as if the place on her back where he touched was suddenly the centre of her entire being, and all of her wanted to be there.

What the...? Could she have an orgasm because someone was touching her?

This was crazy. She was feeling super-sensitive because of the bites. She'd been without sex for far too long.

Surely this had nothing to do with the fact that it was Matt Eveldene who was doing the touching. Surely if an elderly woman with body odour was applying the cream she'd be feeling the same.

Liar, liar, pants on fire. She was face down in her pillow, muffling thoughts, muffling everything, but all she could see was Matt, with his gorgeous dark hair and his long, sensitive fingers doing indescribable things to her, making sure every last part of her back was covered with the anaesthetic cream. Suddenly, dumbly, she found herself wishing she hadn't worn knickers to bed last night and the bites had gone lower.

Uh-oh. She needed to get a grip fast. She was a mature woman, the mother of a seventeen-year-old son, a competent doctor. She did not grip her pillow and stifle groans because some strange man was applying cream to her.

His fingers stopped and to her horror she heard a whimper of protest. Surely that wasn't her?

It was. Was she out of her mind?

But luckily, thankfully, he misinterpreted it. 'These are bad,' he said. 'Kelly, stay still, I'm going to find some ice. I've made them warm again, putting the cream on. We need to get all the heat out of them so you can get some sleep.'

We. Plural. The word was seductive all by itself.

There wasn't a we. There had been never a we.

Matt left and for some stupid reason she found herself thinking of the night Jess had been born. She'd been staying with friends on the far side of the island. They'd promised to be with her for the birth but Jess had come two weeks early. They'd gone out and she'd had no car.

She'd taken the local bus, an hour's bumpy ride in the dark. She'd walked four blocks to the hospital and she'd delivered her baby with no one but too-busy hospital staff in attendance.

Why think of that now?

We. It was the word; it penetrated her deepest thoughts. The only *we* she knew was herself and her son.

And then Matt was back. She hadn't moved. Her world seemed to be doing weird, hazy things. Maybe it was the antihistamines—how much had Matt given her? Or maybe it was the toxic effect of so many bites. No matter, she couldn't have moved if she'd tried. She didn't speak, just lay absolutely still while Matt applied ice packs wrapped in soft cloth to her inflamed skin.

The feeling was incredible. She no longer felt like whimpering. She felt incredibly, amazingly peaceful, like this was right, like this was where she ought to be.

Like this was home.

There was a dumb thought. Home. For her, the concept didn't exist.

'You know, if you rolled over I could ice your front,' Matt said conversationally, and she finally managed to rouse herself.

'In your dreams, Matt Eveldene,' she managed. 'I can ice my front all by myself. Thank you very much. I'll go to sleep now.'

'Are you sure? I can give you—'

'If you give me anything else I'll never wake up. I'm medicated to my eyeballs. Thank you, Matt, and goodnight.'

'Goodnight, Kelly,' he said softly, but he didn't go. For a long moment he simply stood by her bed.

She wanted to roll over. She wanted, quite desperately, to look up at him.

She was naked from the waist up. A girl had to have some sense.

And it seemed Matt had sense, too.

'Goodnight,' he said again, and then, before she knew what he intended—how could she ever have guessed?—he stooped and kissed her lightly on the head.

'You're the bravest woman I've ever met,' he told her. 'Thank you for loving Jessie. It's the greatest gift you could ever have given me.'

'Is that why you kissed me?' she managed, and what sort of question was that? Dumb, she thought, but equally… important.

'No,' he said at last. 'It's not. But it needs to be.'

She was his sister-in-law. Jessie's wife. He had no business thinking of her…as he was thinking.

Why had he kissed her?

It had been a feather kiss, the kiss one might give a child to say goodnight.

It had meant nothing.

Wrong. It had meant…more.

She hadn't felt like Jessie's wife and she hadn't felt like a child. She'd felt—and looked—every inch a woman.

He left the house and walked down to the beach again,

to watch the moon sending its slivers of silver ribbon over the waves. The dogs were silent by his side, as if they knew how important it was that he be given time to think.

There was nothing to think about.

There was everything to think about. A woman called Kelly, a woman lying half-naked in his guest room, a woman responding to his touch…

She had responded. That hadn't been a doctor/patient treatment. The whole room had crackled with sexuality. With need.

His need?

'It's because I'm guilty and grateful,' he said out loud, but he knew it was much, much more.

It couldn't be more. This situation was complicated enough. It didn't need testosterone as well.

'Back off,' he told himself harshly. 'There's so much to be sorted before you can…

'Before you can what?'

Before you can nothing. He raked his hand through his hair and felt weariness envelop him. The family ramifications were enormous. How to let his parents know?

It'd be easier if he didn't. He'd promised Kelly…

But…but…

'Stop it,' he told himself. 'One step at a time. They're both safe now and that's all that matters. She's asleep and you need to take a cold shower.' He was still talking aloud and the dogs were paying attention. Like what he was saying was important.

He looked down at them and gave a rueful chuckle.

'Okay. With the amount of drugs Kelly has on board, she'll sleep until morning, and I need to, too. So go to bed,' he told himself. 'You have a full list in the morning. You have more to think about than Kelly.'

Kelly. Not Jessie's wife. Kelly. It suddenly seemed important to differentiate the two.

The dogs were getting restless. His unease was communicating itself to them. Bess put a tentative paw on his knee and whined.

'Right,' he said, hauling himself together. He picked up a piece of driftwood and hurled it up the track toward the house. Bess bounded after it. Spike looked towards Bess and back toward Matt and whined.

Both dogs were worrying about him.

'Okay, I'm discombobulated,' he told Spike. 'Do you know what that means? No? Well, maybe I don't know either. Maybe all I know is that I need to get on with my life. Home, bed, hospital, medicine. Get your priorities back in line, Eveldene, starting now.'

CHAPTER FIVE

WHEN SHE WOKE, sunshine was pouring in through the open windows. She could hear the waves crashing on the beach below the house.

Two dogs' noses were on her bed.

Bess was so big the dog's nose was practically beside hers. Spike was standing on his haunches, his nose just reaching the top of the mattress.

Both their tails were going like helicopter blades. *Look what we've found—a person! A person in our house!*

She grinned and stretched and it was enough. Spike was up on the bed with her, as if her stretching had been a command. Bess, obviously trained for restraint, stayed where she was. She was sitting and waiting but her tail was still going a mile a minute.

She felt…

She felt…

She glanced at the bedside clock and felt stunned.

Ten o'clock? She'd slept for almost twelve hours!

Visiting hours started at the hospital at ten. She should be there. Jess would be expecting her.

Actually, Jess wouldn't be expecting her. He'd started gentle physio yesterday. She'd supplied him with a week's worth of surfing videos. Talking to his mother would come far down his list of the morning's priorities.

She therefore had nothing to do but lie in this gorgeous bedroom and be sociable to these very nice dogs.

Where was Matt? There was the question and it was a biggie.

It was Monday morning, she told herself. He'd be back in the hospital, where he belonged.

She had his house to herself.

Cautiously she tossed back the covers, apologising to Spike as she did so. 'Sorry, little one. I should have woken earlier and given you more cuddle time.'

But Spike just wiggled and hopped off and headed out the French windows, as if his job had been done. They'd said good morning and now both dogs were off to enjoy the day.

She followed, but only to where the curtains fluttered in the warm breeze. She wasn't exactly respectable. Actually, she wasn't respectable at all. She did a quick rethink and a bit of sheet-wrapping and then dared to explore further.

The dogs were on the veranda.

The view took her breath away.

Wow. Wow, wow and wow. The Pacific Ocean stretched away as far as she could see. The house was nestled in a valley, and the valley broadened out, sweeping down and spreading to a wide, golden beach. Promontories at either end of the beach reached far out to the sea, forming what Kelly thought looked like perfect surf breaks.

The beach looked deserted but civilisation must lie close by, for there were surfers at each headland, drifting on the sun-washed sea, waiting for the right wave.

An ancient cane settee lay along the end of the veranda, covered with saggy cushions and dog hair. Kelly looked at it and thought that of all the perfect places for Jess to convalesce, this was the best.

She'd have to hide the surfboards, though.

Um…what was she thinking? She shouldn't stay here for his whole convalescence.

Why not? Matt was Jessie's uncle. Family. He owed her.

No. He didn't owe her, she reminded herself. He'd been a kid when his brother had died and he'd been shocked and sick. The words he'd flung at her should have been forgiven long ago.

Maybe they had been.

But still she couldn't suppress a grin. If a bit of guilt made it possible for Jess to stay in this place…

Don't try and manipulate. Not Matt.

Involuntarily she tightened her grip on her sheet. What she'd felt last night…

It was only because she'd been exhausted, she told herself, and the mass of bites had been making her feel nauseous. And the antihistamines had been messing with her head.

It was a wonder she hadn't jumped him.

Good grief. She peered cautiously under her sheet, just checking, and saw the welts had subsided. The angry red had faded.

She was still a bit itchy, but it was manageable.

What she needed, though, was coffee. Her apartment might be gorgeous but it didn't have coffee.

Matt must have a kitchen. Matt must be at work.

Matt must have coffee.

The three together were a deal-breaker. Off she went, wearing her sheet. A couple of steps down the veranda she changed her mind, went back and donned the too-thin T-shirt, wound the sheet around her a bit tighter and tried again.

She needn't have bothered. She found Matt's kitchen and it, too, was deserted.

A note lay on the kitchen bench.

Help yourself to anything you need. The keys to the Jeep in the driveway are on top of the fridge. Assuming you have an international driving licence, feel free to use it. Don't forget to drive on the left. The pills in the yellow packet are daytime antihistamines. They won't make you sleepy. Take two. My housekeeper, Mrs Huckle, will be here at ten. I've phoned her and she'll cream your back. I've washed your clothes and they're out in the sun. In this breeze they'll be dry by lunchtime. Take it easy until then. M.

She'd stayed in lots of friends' houses. She'd been left lots of notes. What was it about this one that made her tear up?

He'd done her laundry?

'You must be Kelly.'

She whirled and found a wiry little woman beaming across the room at her. The housekeeper?

'I'm Sally Huckle.' She was in her fifties or early sixties, skinny, sun-worn, wearing skin-tight jeans and a shirt with too much cleavage showing. The woman took her hand and shook it like it might come off.

'A woman on her own,' she said, still beaming. 'Excellent. Too many dratted couples stay here. Only his mother comes by herself and what use is that? He needs a single friend. You're American? And Matt says you have bites. Where's the cream? Matt says you'll need help to put it on and he's told me to apply ice packs as well. Talk about orders. And if you weren't awake I wasn't to wake you but when you did could I please make you pancakes for breakfast.'

She beamed, and her beam was widely enquiring. 'I'm not Matt's friend,' Kelly said stiffly, before the woman could keep going. 'I'm his sister-in-law.'

'His sister-in-law?'

If Jess was coming here to stay, why not say it? 'Yes. My son's had an accident on the Gold Coast. He's still in hospital but he's coming back here to convalesce.'

'Your son? You're Matt's sister-in-law?' The woman sounded incredulous. 'You're Jessie's wife?'

'I… Yes.'

'Your son is Jessie's son?'

'Yes.' Where was she landing herself?

'Does his father know about you?'

'No.'

'Then God help you when he finds out,' she said bluntly. 'Are you sure it's a good idea to stay here?'

'Matt doesn't seem to have given me much choice.' She hesitated. 'But what's wrong with his father knowing?'

'Do you know about your father-in-law?'

'Not much.'

'Then take a look,' the woman said, and crossed to an alcove holding a desktop computer. 'I'm just the hired help but everyone in Australia knows about the Eveldenes.' She hit the browser and in seconds Henry Eveldene's face filled the screen.

'This was written as a Sunday papers feature a couple of years back,' Sally said. 'As far as I can figure, it's accurate. Take a read while I make pancakes. The man makes my hair stand on end. I've never met him but Matt's mother comes here while he's overseas and that's enough. Downtrodden's too big a word for it. Sit. Read.'

'I don't need pancakes.'

'Matt might not be as scary as his father,' Sally said, 'but he's my boss. He's still an Eveldene and what he says goes. Sit. Read. Pancakes.'

Two hours later Kelly was driving cautiously—why didn't the whole world drive on the right?—trying to take in everything she'd learned about Matt's family.

Jessie's family, she reminded herself. Henry Eveldene was Jessie's grandfather.

He was also a giant of industry, owning and operating a huge consortium of paper mills.

He was also a greedy, avaricious bully.

The page Sally had found for her to read had pulled no punches. It spoke of a man to whom money was second only to power. He operated on a knife edge between legal and illegal. He coerced, bullied, blackmailed, and his competitors had gone under one by one.

The article hadn't stopped at his dubious business practices, though. It had talked of the beautiful, wealthy girl he'd married, and how she'd faded from sight and was now practically a recluse.

The article was careful. Kelly could see litigation concerns all over it, but the implications were everywhere. It described two sons, the expectation that they'd move into the family dynasty and take orders from their father, the older son's breakdown and suicide, the younger son's decision to move into medicine, and the subsequent estrangement.

The picture emerged of a solitary megalomaniac who tried to destroy everyone who opposed him.

What would he do if he discovered he had a grandson?

She shivered and went back to concentrating on the road. Stupid left-hand drivers.

But this was a cool little Jeep, fitted with roll bars to

make it into a dune buggy. She could have fun with this machine.

She scolded herself. It wasn't hers.

Hey, but it was, for the time she was staying with Matt. She had visions of putting Jess in the back seat and heading out to explore the local coast. There were places she'd read about around here where they could drive on the beach. They could look for surf spots where they could return once his leg was healed.

Jess's convalescence was looking a lot brighter because of Matt.

Matt… An enigma. Matt, who caused her stomach to clench and she couldn't figure out why.

Matt, who'd done her laundry. Matt, who'd put cream on her back last night, who'd kissed her hair and who'd made her feel

Enough. She didn't feel like that. She was solid, sensible Dr Kelly Eveldene and if only she could avoid the odd oncoming car she was off to visit her recuperating son and live happily ever after.

Matt's theatre list took him all morning and into the afternoon. He finished at two, rid himself of his theatre scrubs, figured he needed to do a ward round but first he'd grab a sandwich. Maybe he'd take it up to Jessie's ward to eat.

Was it wise to get any closer to Jess? Maybe it wasn't but the decision had been taken out of his hands the moment he'd offered accommodation to Kelly. Besides, he had a nephew. The thought was unnerving but it wasn't something that'd go away.

The minute he'd seen him he'd known this was Jessie's son. Now, come hell or high water, he'd look out for him.

And if he was to look out for him then he needed to get to know him.

As an uncle.

As a friend to his mother?

He'd look out for Kelly, too, but it wasn't just because Jess had married her. It seemed more.

Except he couldn't define more.

He pushed open Jess's door, balancing sandwiches and coffee. Two faces turned to him. Jess and Kelly.

Jess was so like his father that it made Matt's heart twist.

Kelly was so like…Kelly that for some stupid reason his heart twisted even further.

'Hi,' Jess said shyly. 'Come in.'

'I'm not here on business,' he told them. 'No poking and prodding, unless there are any problems?'

'No problems,' Jess said. 'But thank you for looking after my mom.'

That took his breath away. So someone else was looking out for Kelly.

'I told her yesterday she had to get out of that crappy apartment,' Jess said. 'Thanks for picking her up and forcing her.'

'Do you need to pick her up and force her often?' Matt asked, and Jess grinned.

'If you only knew. She's stubborn as a brick, my mom. Immovable. And stupid about money. She has some dumb idea—'

'Jess!' Kelly intervened. 'Let's not be telling Dr Eveldene our family business.'

'Yeah, but Dr Eveldene *is* our family,' Jess said, shy again. 'Isn't that right, sir?'

'I… Yes. But not so much of the "sir".'

'Uncle Matt?'

'Matt.' The uncle bit did his head in.

'Take a seat,' Jess said, relaxing. 'We're watching the next leg of the surf circuit in New Zealand. This guy coming up next is pretty good. He's getting a bit old, though. I reckon his knees might start crumbling soon.'

'How old is a bit old?' Matt asked, perching on the spare visitor's chair.

'Twenty-eight,' Jess said, and Matt choked on his coffee and grinned and looked across at Kelly and found she was grinning as well.

'Yep, you and I are well and truly on the scrap heap,' she said. 'It's a wonder we can still see our knees.'

'Speak for yourself. I do push-ups,' Matt told her. 'Every morning. I reckon I'll be able to see my knees until I'm at least fifty.'

'Dream on,' Kelly said, grinning back. 'Knees don't exist when you're fifty.'

'Especially old knees in neoprene,' Jess said, and shuddered. 'Old guys in wetsuits…ugh.'

'Thank you,' Kelly said with asperity. 'Shall we talk about something else? Like when Dr Eveldene will let you out of hospital?'

'Call me Matt,' Matt said sharply.

'Matt,' Kelly said, as if making a concession, but then she smiled and he thought…he thought…

Concentrate on Jess, he told himself. Concentrate on what mattered. Jess was his family. Kelly wasn't.

'The vascular surgeon and I concur, a week in hospital,' Matt managed. 'And we talked yesterday about surfing. You know it'll be six months before you can safely surf again. Have you had any thoughts about what you might do while you convalesce?'

This was a conversation he often had with patients. As an orthopaedic surgeon, he often treated people with passions—paragliders, trail bike riders, skiers, people who pushed their bodies to extremes.

Not fronting that question—What will you do while your body recovers?—was an invitation to depression, and with Jessie's family background there was no way Matt was ignoring the risk.

'I'll sulk,' Jess said, with an attempt at lightness that didn't quite come off. He saw Kelly glance at her son sharply and then look away. So she was worried, too.

'When did you leave school?' Matt asked. 'If you're interested, you might be able to go back for a bit. A couple of subjects might hold you in good stead if you decide you need a career when your knees go.'

There was silence in the room. His suggestion had been presumptuous, Matt knew, but, then…his big brother had had nothing but surfing. To see this kid go the same way…

'I've done with schooling for a while,' Jess said, turning back to the surfing on television. 'Mom and I made a deal. No more study.'

What sort of deal was that—letting your son do nothing but surf? But he'd pushed the boundaries as far as he could. Mother and son both suddenly seemed tense and there was no way he could take it further.

'I might learn to play snakes and ladders,' Jess said, attempting lightness but his words weren't light at all.

'I'll buy you a set,' Matt told him. 'No,' he said, as his offer was met by silence. He put up his hands as if to ward off protests. 'I insist. As an uncle it's the only appropriate thing to do.'

Jess chuckled and went back to watching what the surfer was doing on television. Kelly cast him a look of relief and Matt unwrapped his sandwich and wondered where to go next. What was the role of an uncle?

And then his phone went.

Of course. This was part of his job. How many times had meals been interrupted by his phone? At least this was just a sandwich.

He tossed Kelly an apologetic glance—no need to

send one to Jess, who was engrossed again in his surfing world—and answered.

Trouble.

He tossed his sandwich in the bin and headed for the door.

'What?' Kelly demanded.

'Work.'

'Yeah, but it's a biggie,' she said. 'I'm a doctor, too, remember? I know the drill. If you get a minor call, you rewrap your sandwich. You ditched your sandwich so I'm figuring it's major. I shouldn't ask but—'

'Bus crash,' he said curtly. 'A self-drive bus of tourists mucking about off road in the sand dunes. They copped a head-on with a council grader on the far side of a crest. Deaths and multiple casualties. We'll be pushing to get staff to cover it. See you tomorrow, Jess.'

'Matt, can I help?' Kelly asked sharply.

'I don't see how.' He had the door open; he needed to leave.

'Matt, as surf-pro physician I have provisional registration to work in almost every country we visit,' she said, talking fast. 'In emergencies I can stay hands on. In hospitals I require overall supervision from local medics, but I'm a doctor, I'm another pair of hands and I'm available. Do you need me?'

Matt hesitated. An unknown doctor, overseas trained…

But this accident involved twenty or more tourists, Beth had said, and she'd sounded desperate. They were evacuating some to Brisbane but there was only one chopper and most were coming by road. This was the first and only place that casualties could be stabilised.

He steadied. He did know her. He trusted her. He needed to check, though, for the sake of the patients she'd be treating.

'Can you prove your registration?'

'My paperwork's in my travel wallet with my gear at your place,' she told him, as if she'd expected the question. She hauled a card from her purse. 'But you can ring this number. Quote my name and my registration number. They'll confirm fast.'

She'd done this before, he thought. She'd acted as a doctor in a foreign setting. Then, he thought, *of course she had.* Kelly—or the organisation she worked for—would have set up temporary registration from the moment she entered the country, so in an emergency, if there weren't enough medics on hand, she could act as a doctor without repercussions.

'Phone while we hit the lift,' she said.

'Thank you.' There was nothing else to say.

They left Jess to his surfing and headed for Emergency. They didn't speak on the way down. He'd phoned and was listening to someone in officialdom telling him Kelly was fine.

A small army seemed to be waiting for them, but they were mostly nurses. Matt glanced around and saw only three qualified doctors, Beth, Frieda and Emma. Beth and Frieda were good but Emma had only passed her final exams last month. She wasn't confident at the best of times, and now she was looking terrified.

'I'm trying to get more hands here,' Beth told him as she saw his visual sweep of the room and guessed his thoughts. 'But everyone seems to be in the middle of something urgent. Brisbane's on standby. We're pulling in another chopper, but for now it's down to us.'

'Kelly's offered to help. She's an emergency physician accredited for work here under supervision. I've done the checks.'

'Excellent,' Beth said with relief. 'Matt, can you do a fast tour, show her what's needed and find her some scrubs. Kelly, can I put you on triage with Rachel, our senior nurse? Direct the straightforward ones to Emma, the harder ones to the rest of us.'

Kelly nodded. Matt saw her assessing the teams of nurses, checking the doctors, then glancing at Emma, who looked like she was about to faint.

'Maybe Emma and I could work together,' Kelly suggested. 'With Rachel's help, we could do triage and urgent stabilisation as a team. I'm supposed to work under supervision if Australian doctors are present so it'd cover all the bases.' Then, as Emma visibly relaxed at the thought of not working alone, Kelly moved on. 'Do you have an anaesthetist?'

'That's Frieda,' Matt told her, signalling to a grey-haired woman currently tossing orders to nurses on the other side of the room. 'If we need 'em, intubation and tracheotomies are her specialty.'

'I can do trachies in my sleep.' Frieda threw her a friendly grin. 'We're always short-staffed, but this is looking crazy hard. Glad to have another Eveldene on board.' She gave a brief smile.

'I hope you don't need me,' Kelly told her, but then the scream of an ambulance outside announced the first arrival and there was room for no more talk.

They needed Kelly. They needed everyone.

This was war-zone stuff.

Kelly had trained as an emergency physician. She'd done mock-ups of this type of scenario but she'd never been in one. Nevertheless, her drilled-in training kicked in, making her reactions instinctive. By her side the very junior Emma was visibly shaking. Emma supervising Kelly? Ha!

The first arrival, a girl of about sixteen, had a deep gash running from under her arm to the small of her back.

Her blood pressure was dangerously low—the drip wasn't going fast enough. The other casualty coming through was a spinal injury with breathing difficulties. Matt and Frieda took that case, while Beth headed out to greet whoever was coming next.

That was almost the last time Kelly had time to see what everyone else was doing. She focused only on the kid under her hands.

She reached for the adrenaline, showed Rachel—thankfully capable—where to apply pressure, and snapped orders to Emma. 'Get another line in. We need as much fluid as we can.'

Emma's hands shook as she tried to do as ordered.

'Stop,' Kelly said, grabbed the young woman's hands and held for one harsh moment. 'Deep breath. Emma, you will not mess this up. You can't. The only wrong way is not at all. You know how to do this. Move to automatic pilot. Don't think of the consequences. You've had years of training. This is what you're here for, Emma. Do it.'

And Emma met her gaze, took a deep breath and visibly steadied. She picked up the syringe and inserted it into the back of the girl's hand. It went exactly where it was supposed to go and she didn't even pause for breath before turning to grab bags of plasma.

From fifteen feet away, where Matt and Frieda were working on a woman who probably wouldn't make it but had to be given every chance, Matt saw and felt a jab of relief. Yeah, he'd watched. He had too much on his plate, but he'd assured Beth that Kelly was qualified. Lives were in her hands and it would have been negligent not do a fast visual check.

Two minutes in he was completely reassured. Not only did she work like an efficient machine but she'd settled Emma, so instead of one terrified novice, they had a team of two steady, intent doctors.

'It has to be cervical spine fracture,' Frieda barked. 'Get her straight through to Imaging.'

And then the woman's shallow breathing ceased. Kelly was forgotten, everything was forgotten as they fought to get her back—and lost.

And when they surfaced from defeat there were more casualties waiting. A couple more doctors arrived. The department looked even more like a war zone.

He lost sight of Kelly. He lost sight of everything except trying to save lives.

CHAPTER SIX

BY NINE THAT night there was nothing left for Kelly to do. Patients had been transferred, to Theatre, to wards, to other hospitals at need. A couple were in the morgue.

That was a gut wrenching she could never get used to. In emergency situations Kelly worked on the front line, but eventually surgeons, anaesthetists, paediatricians, neurologists, even grief counsellors, moved in and took over.

But sometimes Kelly thought she needed counselling herself. She felt like that now, but she'd done what she'd needed to do. When the last patient was wheeled out, Beth thanked her and told her to go home.

'We wouldn't have had the outcome we did without you,' she told her. 'And the way you hauled Emma together…your help today meant we had five doctors instead of three.'

'Emma's a good doctor,' Kelly said, wishing, stupidly, that Matt was still here, but Matt was an orthopaedic surgeon, one of those who kept working after emergency imperatives had been met. He'd probably be operating until morning.

'She's good *now*,' Beth told her. 'Thanks to you, she worked well, and she'll never be as terrified again. And as for you, if you'd like part-time work while you and Jessie are stuck here, just say the word. It'd be a huge pleasure to have two Eveldenes working in this hospital.'

Two Eveldenes… That was a weird concept.

She and Matt.

Something was twisting inside her. What?

Today she'd been part of Matt's team. Matt had vouched for her and she'd worked in his hospital. Beth was referring to them as the two Eveldenes.

Strangely it felt like she had family, and the feeling was weird.

She found herself wishing she could go home with Matt now. She'd seen him as they'd wheeled the last patient out of Emergency to Theatre. He was facing multiple fractures. He'd be working all night.

And he'd looked haggard already.

He was nothing to do with her.

Wrong. He was an Eveldene.

Family?

Needing to ground herself, she headed back to Jessie's room. Jess was deeply asleep. She sat by his bed, just watching him. Settling herself in her son's presence.

After a while the nurse in charge of the ward popped in. 'I've been sent to take care of you,' she said, efficiency overlaid with kindness. 'Would you like tea and a sandwich? Or something hot? The whole hospital knows what you've done today and we're grateful. We can heat you some soup if you like. Anything.'

'Thank you, no.' She rose, feeling bone weary. There was no point in staying here. 'I need to go home.'

'And you're staying with Matt. You're his sister-in-law, the wife of his brother who died. That's awfully sad.'

'It was a long time ago,' Kelly said repressively, but knowing hospital grapevines were the same the world over. She had as much chance of hiding her history as flying.

'But still…' The woman glanced at Jess. 'They say he's

just like his dad, and you've brought him up in America but finally you've brought him home.'

'This isn't home.'

'You just said it was,' the woman said gently. 'And we all think you're wonderful already. If Jess needs an uncle and you need roots, why not stay? Heaven knows, Matt needs a family.'

'Matt has a family.' She was sounding curt to the point of rudeness now but the woman wasn't noticing. What was it about the medical world that made its inhabitants think they could intrude into their colleagues' lives? It happened the world over and here was obviously no exception.

'One failed marriage, one wimp of a mother and one bully of a father,' the nurse said softly, thoughtfully. 'The whole hospital's been trying to get our Matt paired off for ever. We'd practically given up.'

'I'm his sister-in-law, not a potential girlfriend,' Kelly snapped, and the nurse grinned.

'Of course you are,' she agreed. 'But as you said yourself, all that was a long time ago. And our Dr Matt is gorgeous.'

Our Dr Matt is gorgeous.

The problem was that he was.

Kelly drove home in the dark. She normally needed all her attention to stay on the left, but the road was quiet and there was a fraction of her mind free to stray.

She'd been acutely aware of Matt today. Beth was in charge of Emergency but she'd almost unconsciously deferred to Matt. He'd worked like two men, one part working to salvage mangled limbs, the other watching what was going on in the rest of the room. He'd snapped curt orders, not just for the patient he was treating but for others as well. He didn't interfere with any other doctor's treatment, but he was covering the room, making sure equipment, plasma, saline, everything needed was on hand.

Supply should have been a full-time role but there hadn't been enough medical hands on deck to cover it. Matt had done it seamlessly, as well as ensuring at least two people didn't need amputation. As well as reassuring frightened patients. As well as fielding a call from the overseas parents of the girl who'd died under his hands. The hospital counsellors had moved in to take most of the calls but for that one the counsellor had approached him.

'They know their daughter didn't die instantly. They have visions of her dying in agony. Matt, if you could…'

Matt could. He'd stepped to a corner of the room near where Kelly had been working and she'd heard him speaking, quietly, gently, as if he'd had all the time in the world.

'With the blow to the head as well as the spinal injury she'd have been instantly unconscious and not frightened or in any pain. Apparently they were having a wonderful time in the bus. It started slipping on the dunes and everyone thought it was fun. The passengers thought it was supposed to happen, so there was no terror. Yes, she was alive when she was brought into hospital but the paramedics assure me she was deeply unconscious from the moment of impact.'

And then… 'No. I'm so sorry but even if we'd been able to save her, her brain damage would have been massive and the spinal injury would have meant total paralysis. Of course I'm available to answer any questions you might have in the future, and certainly if you decide to come to Australia to take your girl home, I'll talk to you then. Or before. That goes for any of our staff. The paramedics who brought her in, the counsellors, any one of the men and women who've cared for her, we're all here for you.'

Kelly hadn't been able to hear the other end of the conversation but she'd listened to Matt's reassurances and she'd thought somewhere on the other side of the world devastated parents would put down the phone knowing everything that could have been done for their girl had been done.

She'd been in caring hands.

Caring…

She thought of the Matt she'd met eighteen years ago. Caring was the last word she'd have thought to apply to him.

That had been a long time ago. So…what?

Her thoughts were drifting and she wasn't sure where. Or maybe she did know but it scared her. She needed to think of someone…of something else.

She'd been offered a job. That was a good thought. If she could work and earn, maybe she wouldn't have to stay in Matt's house.

But Jess would love staying in Matt's house, and Matt was Jessie's uncle. Did she have the right to refuse to let them get to know each other? A week ago she'd have said yes. After tonight, seeing Matt's skill, seeing Matt's inherent kindness, she thought: possibly not.

But where did that leave her? The way she was feeling… Matt's skill and kindness was doing her head in.

Was that down to his likeness to her husband?

Possibly not, she thought. She'd been widowed for eighteen years and her memories of her husband had been obscured by time. He was a loving ghost at her shoulder, but he wasn't one who reminded her to mourn. Neither was he one who claimed ownership.

He'd be troubled that she'd never had another serious relationship, she thought, and she struggled to conjure him up. What would his advice be?

Do what's right for today, Kell, he'd say. *Don't let tomorrow's monsters scare you. Tomorrow they'll look like*

*minnows. You can kick them away with the pleasure you
gain from today. Especially from today's surf.*

Maybe she needed a surf.

Now? In the dark?

Maybe not.

What she needed now was bed. What she needed now
was to make the confusion in her head go away.

'You'll all be minnows tomorrow,' she told her doubts,
but the image of Matt on the telephone superimposed itself.

There was no way Matt Eveldene would ever be a min-
now.

Matt slept badly. He always did after tragedy. While he'd
trained he'd thought eventually he'd get used to it but he
never had. The anger at the waste of life, because one un-
skilled driver had thought it would be fun to gun a busload
of kids over cresting sand dunes... The grief it caused...
The grief that would go on and on...

Like the grief he felt for his brother.

He thought of the woman presumably sleeping just
through the wall from him and the grief she'd endured.
He could have helped her.

There was yet more grief.

He found himself thinking of his mother in that appalling mausoleum of a house, afraid to walk away from her
husband, afraid of her own shadow. But maybe she wasn't
afraid, he thought. Maybe she couldn't escape grief wherever she went, so why try? He brought her here when his
father was away but she was totally passive. She sat on the
veranda and stared out to sea, and as soon as her husband
was due home, she packed and left.

He'd tried to persuade her to seek help. He'd made ap-
pointments for her with psychologists, but no one had been
able to break through.

Could Kelly?

Could Jessie?

There was another worry keeping him awake. If he let his mother know of Jessie's existence, it'd bring joy, but it'd also set loose the full force of his father. Kelly was one strong woman but no one could face down his father.

He slept fitfully, and finally it was dawn. He dropped a hand to greet the dogs at the side of his bed—and found nothing.

Traitors, he thought, remembering they hadn't bounded out to greet him last night either. They'd be with Kelly.

They'd be just through the wall. By her bed.

This was driving him crazy. He'd head down to the beach before work, he decided. At least the waves might clear the fog.

He grabbed his swimmers, headed out to the veranda and paused.

Someone was surfing just below the house. His dogs were on the beach, standing guard as they did when he surfed.

He gazed along the veranda to where two surfboards usually lay, one short and light for when he wanted to push himself, the other a long board, stable and easy to paddle, for times when he wanted to lie behind the breakers and catch the occasional wave with ease.

The small one was gone. It took skill...

She had skill.

He stood and watched in the soft dawn light. A rolling breaker was coming in. The sea was silk smooth, glimmering in the sun's early rays. The breaker was a dark shadow, moving swiftly, building height as it neared the shallows.

She caught its force at just the right time, at just the right angle. In one smooth movement she was on her feet, sleek and light, her feet at one with the board, working it like a lover.

She wasn't content to simply ride the wave to shore. She

crested to the lip and swooped, she flipped a turn, then cruised under the breaking foam. Finally she dropped full length, dipping her head so the wave wouldn't push her backwards, and started paddling, easily and smoothly, out to catch the next wave.

She was wearing a simple black costume. Her hair was a tangle of dripping curls. She looked…she looked…

No. There were a hundred reasons why he shouldn't think how she was looking.

He thought of how she'd been when Jess had found her. Seventeen. She'd been a wild creature, he thought. Maybe she still was.

Why would he prefer to see her as a wild creature? Someone who could never fit into a life like this?

Still, she shouldn't be surfing alone.

He glanced across at the headlands and was almost disappointed to see other surfers in the water. It was an unwritten rule that surfers looked out for others when they could see them. She wasn't actually alone.

But now she'd seen him. He must be obvious, standing on the veranda, watching.

He didn't want to intrude but she waved as if she was including him in her morning—and then the next wave rolled in and she went back to concentrating on the surf.

How could he resist? He couldn't. He had two hours before he needed to leave for work and Kelly was surfing on his beach. Even his dogs were waiting.

Putting away the hundred reasons why he shouldn't, he grabbed his long board and went to join her.

For Kelly, surfing was as natural as breathing. It was her release, her escape. She surfed with friends, she surfed with Jess, but their presence didn't matter.

It was also okay to surf with Matt, for he understood silence.

She'd met chatty surfers and they drove her crazy. It was okay to lie out behind the waves and solve the problems of the world after a long morning's surf, but to choose to talk rather than surf…

Matt didn't. He simply paddled out to her, raised a hand in greeting and concentrated on the next wave.

He caught it with ease, rose, steadied, then manoeuvred the big board with skill and rode it until the wave shrank into the shallows.

A surfing surgeon.

He wasn't as skilled as a pro, but he was more than competent. He was riding a big old board, because she had his good one. He looked good on it. No, he looked great. She'd thought he was married to his medicine but his body was tanned and ripped and he couldn't be as good as this without practice.

A wave swelled and swept past—and she'd missed it. It was a beauty. Matt caught it and in seconds he was in the green room, that gorgeous sapphire tube of perfectly looped water.

If he'd had his good board he could have stayed in there for the length of the ride. As it was, he emerged and glanced back at her and said, 'If you're going to waste waves like that, I want my board back.'

She chuckled and glanced behind and caught the next one, and somehow things had changed between them again.

Something had settled.

This was her husband's brother, she told herself as the morning grew brighter, as they caught wave after wave, as the silence deepened and strengthened between them. He was Jess's uncle.

But she knew, at some deep level, he was becoming much, much more.

It should scare her, but it didn't. She rode her waves and Matt rode behind, before or beside her, and it didn't matter.

Something had changed. Somehow, for this moment, she felt peace.

The morning had to end. Matt had patients waiting. 'Stay if you want,' Matt told her, but she shook her head. In truth, she wasn't as fit as she used to be. Two hours' surfing was enough.

'Do you want to leave the boards in the dunes?' Matt said. 'The surfers at the headlands never come this far. No one comes along here but us. You...*we* could surf tomorrow.'

There was a promise. She managed a wavery smile in return.

'The short one's yours tomorrow.'

'No way. My skills don't match yours. Right now I can blame the board and that's the way I like it.'

She chuckled and they headed up to the house.

If I was a teenager I might reach out and take his hand, Kelly thought, and then hauled herself back under control.

Yeah, but you're not a teenager. You have a whole lot more hormones—and Matt needs to go to work.

Matt.

But...but...

'You're smiling because...?' Matt asked, and she found herself blushing from the toes up.

'Yeah,' Matt said. 'Me, too.'

Me, too? Really? *Really*?

'Not appropriate,' she managed.

'No.'

Okay. That was decided.

'Not when I have a theatre list in forty minutes.'

Hmm. There was enough promise in that statement to take a woman's breath away. 'You get first shower,' she told him, feeling suddenly breathless. 'Unless there's enough water pressure for two showers.'

'There's not," he said.

"Go. I'll make breakfast.'

'I'll grab a coffee at the hospital.'

'You can't surf for hours and then operate on an empty stomach. Surgeon fainting mid-list? Not a good look.'

'Toast, then,' he said, and she nodded.

'Toast. Go.'

'Kelly?'

But his nearness was doing things to her. He was too big, too broad, too almost naked. His chest was still wet. Water was still dripping from his hair. He looked...

'Toast,' she said, and if she sounded desperate, who could blame her? 'But shower, now. Go!'

He ran his shower cold. Really cold. If he could have added ice it would have been a sensible option. He dressed with care, thinking it'd be better if he was consulting rather than operating this morning because then he could dress formally in suit. He could always take his jacket off later, but for some reason it seemed imperative that he be completely, carefully dressed when he saw Kelly again. If he didn't have a suit jacket and tie on it would be so easy to...

No. Any minute now it'd be another cold shower.

Breakfast. Toast. He headed for his kitchen, thinking he should have made it clear to Kelly that he'd eat on his side and she could do whatever she wanted on her side, but he hadn't made it clear and he copped the smell of eggs and bacon before he got there. *In his kitchen.*

Kelly was frying bacon. She had a beach towel wrapped round her like a sarong. Her feet were still sandy. Her curls were tangled damply around her shoulders.

Every part of him froze.

Every part of him wanted.

No. A man had to work!

Sensibly, though, a man also had to have breakfast. Treat this as ordinary, he pleaded with himself. He walked in and she turned and smiled at him and handed him a loaded plate of eggs, bacon, fried tomato and toast.

'A boy's fantasies are all coming together right here,' he managed. He had the plate in his hands. That helped. He couldn't reach out and touch her. But she was still too close and that towel was tucked simply into itself right at her breast and he knew underneath was that simple slip of black Lycra…

'Seduction by bacon,' she said demurely. 'Things your mother never taught you.'

'No.' He hesitated, trying to figure how to get this electric charge out of the room. History, he thought. Remember bleakness. 'Your mother never taught you much by the sound of it,' he tried.

'No,' she said, and the smile slipped a little. 'But I've been around enough surf camps in my life to know a great feed after surfing is a sure way to a man's heart. You'll still have forgotten me by lunchtime, though. You'll see. The lady in the cafeteria will smile at you as she hands you your turkey sandwich and you'll change allegiances, just like that.'

He thought of Tilda in the hospital canteen, fair, fat and fifty. He looked again at Kelly's bare toes and the sand in her cleavage and the way one curl was just trailing downward…

'I think you just won,' he said, and he couldn't keep his voice steady.

'Love's more fickle than you think,' Kelly said serenely, turning back to cook her own breakfast.

'You mean no one ever fell for you after Jessie?' He tried to keep the question casual—and failed.

'Sure they did,' she said. 'I've cooked so many breakfasts I couldn't possibly count.'

'Kelly...'

She turned. The bacon sizzled in the pan behind her. She looked at him.

'I don't do light stuff,' she said in a voice that was anything but light. 'My dad was promiscuous, living with woman after woman after woman. I'm Jessie's mother. That comes first. It always has and it always will.'

'Jess is growing up.'

'And he still needs to respect his mom.'

'How can he not respect you?'

'Eat your breakfast,' she told him, and deliberately turned away. She finished cooking hers, served it out and then sat on the opposite side of the table. They ate in silence. Things were happening between them, and he didn't have a clue what.

I don't do light stuff. It was a warning to back off.

He didn't—necessarily—want to back off, but the complications of falling for this woman were immense.

Was he falling for her?

Had he already fallen?

He'd only known her a few days. She was his brother's wife.

'I need to go,' he managed, thinking he needed space, and, thank heaven, medicine could supply it. 'I'm doing Gloria Matterson's hip replacement this morning. She's been waiting for two years in the public queue and she doesn't need to wait longer.'

'Of course you do. And this... Maybe this morning wasn't a good idea,' Kelly told him.

And he thought, she needs space, too.

What was happening between them? Exactly nothing. They hadn't even kissed.

He rose and carted his plate to the sink. He'd have coffee on the way to work. There was a drive-through…

He turned and Kelly had risen with her plate and she was just…there. Right in front of him.

She looked adorable.

He took the plate from her grasp and put it in the sink behind him. He did it without turning. For some reason it seemed imperative that he didn't break their locked gazes.

I don't do light stuff.

This wasn't light. This was a force he'd never felt before, a sensual pull stronger than any he'd ever known. He wanted to take the beach towel and tug it to the floor. He wanted to run his hands over the curve of her beautiful hips. He wanted…

He'd just have to want. Gloria Matterson wanted, too, and she'd have been given pre-op drugs already.

'I need to go,' he said hoarsely.

'Of course you do.'

'Kelly…'

'Just go.'

'I will,' he said, and if it sounded like a vow, maybe it was. Then, because he couldn't help himself, because there was no way he could stop himself, he took her shoulders in his hands, drew her to him and kissed her.

She should not be kissing Matt Eveldene. Not!

For eighteen years she'd hated this man. She'd hated his family, she'd hated everything he represented. She'd sworn never to have anything to do with him or his ghastly family ever in her lifetime. And now she was in his arms, her mouth was on his, and she was being soundly, solidly kissed.

No. Not soundly. Not solidly. There was nothing about those two words that came near to describing what was happening to her right now.

She was being…subsumed.

Was that the word? Actually, who cared? His mouth was warm on hers, his hands were hugging her close, her breasts were moulding against him and the kiss…oh, the kiss…

It felt like fire. It felt like pure, hot fusion. She could taste him, feel him, melt into him.

He was large and strong and sure. The soft wool of his gorgeous suit was whispering against the bare skin of her shoulders. His hands were in the small of her back, pressing her closer. His strong, angular face was hard against hers.

Her hands rose seemingly of their own accord and ran through his thick, black hair to tug him closer, close enough so she felt their mouths were welded together, a fusion growing stronger by the moment.

As was the heat building through her body. She was on fire.

She wanted this man, right here, right now, but he was already putting her away because Gloria Matterson was waiting and there were medical imperatives and this was… this was…

Crazy.

Her towel slipped. It lay in a puddle on the floor and she thought of what might have happened if there had been no surgical list waiting. She could…

She couldn't. Somehow she managed a deep breath. Yes, that's what she had to do. Recover, think things through and get on with…what she had to get on with.

'Uh-oh,' she managed, but she didn't quite recognise the husky whisper that came out. 'I knew my cooking was good but not that good.'

'There's a lot about you that's good.'

'You…don't know me.'

'There is that. We should have started this as online dating. I'd know your star sign then.'

'So what's yours?' She wasn't making sense, even to herself.

'Libra.'

'Uh-oh. I'm Aries. I'll walk all over you. Favourite music?'

'Wagner.'

'Really?' She choked.

'Um, no.' He grinned, lightening the room with his devastating smile. 'Assuming this is online dating data, I threw that in to scare away the hip-hops. But classical, yes.'

'But mine *is* hip-hop,' she said mournfully, trying to smile back, carefully retrieving her towel and rewrapping it. 'So we're doomed from the start. Take this no further, Dr Eveldene. Go to work.'

'Until tonight?'

'I should move out,' she said worriedly. 'I don't think—'

'Don't move out.'

'Because?'

'Because I don't want you to.' His smile faded. He cupped her chin in his hand and kissed her again, hard and fast. 'You're right, we don't know each other. We have baggage that is certain to get in the way. Hip-hop, classic—problem, but there are always earphones. Kelly...my home is special and I wish to share it with you. Please stay.'

'I'll stay,' she said, and he had to go. She stood and watched as he headed out the door, into his car and out of sight. Her hand stayed on her lips as if she could keep the taste of him just by holding it there.

He disappeared and reality set in. But not regret.

She'd just kissed her husband's brother. For years she'd regarded him as the enemy. Kissing him should have seemed like a betrayal and yet...it hadn't. It had felt right.

More, it felt like the bitterness that had stayed with her

for all those years had melted in that kiss. Ultimate forgiveness? Ultimate moving on?

But what had he said? *My home is special.* It was an odd line for a guy to use. Seduction by interior design?

She glanced about her at his stunning home. She glanced into the living room at the great rock mantelpiece, the exquisite rugs, the floor-to-ceiling windows framing the ocean beyond.

My home is special.

'I'd have stayed anyway,' she whispered, still touching her lips. 'The way you kissed me seems to have wiped away the awfulness of the past. And in such a kiss, I might not have noticed your home.'

She hardly noticed places. No, that wasn't true. She could certainly appreciate that Matt's house was beautiful. It was just that she saw houses—homes—as transient.

My home is special...

It was such an odd statement that she found herself thinking again of the inherent, basic differences between them. Classic, hip-hop. Aries, Libra. Nomad, house-loving. Internet dating wouldn't have stood a chance.

My home is special...

She thought back eighteen years, to her beloved Jess, trying to explain about his family.

'All my dad ever thinks about is things. His home. His possessions.'

Jess had rejected those things and so had she.

'Dad controls people with his possessions,' Jess had told her. *'We don't need them.'*

She still didn't. She'd been fiercely independent all her life, and nothing was changing now. Just because one man had kissed her...

Oh, for heaven's sake. Stop worrying, she told herself crossly. She should take a shower and then head to the hospital. She had a son to visit. Beth had promised to talk to her about a job. She had enough to do today without thinking of possessions controlling her. She had enough to do without thinking of the incompatibility between the two Drs Eveldene.

And in any gaps in her day, qualms or not, she had a kiss to remember.

CHAPTER SEVEN

'How about triage in Emergency?' To say Beth was enthusiastic about employing her was an understatement. 'The local surf competitions come straight after the world tour so we're overrun with surfing casualties. Plus, it's school holidays, which always sees us busy. Could you work mornings from eight to one? That's when most surf casualties come in. Your provisional registration means you're supposed to be supervised, but with your skills I'm happy to supervise from half a hospital away. From what I gather, you can cope with most surf injuries in your sleep.'

So it was settled. Excellent. Wasn't it?

How had her life changed so dramatically? She was living in Matt's house. She was working in Matt's hospital.

She'd been kissing in Matt's kitchen.

Giving in to temptation...

Um, temptation wasn't exactly what she needed to be considering, when the woman in front of her was offering her a job.

'I coped with a kid impaled on a surfboard once,' Kelly told her, trying hard to feel and sound professional. 'A grommit—a learner surfer—thought it'd be a great idea to make his surfboard stand out. He drew the eyes and the razor teeth of a swordfish and whittled the snout to a sharp point. He came off, his leg rope jerked him onto the point and the whole thing went through his thigh. He came into ER with fibreglass still attached.'

'Yikes,' Beth said. 'Happy ending?'

'A textbook surfboard-ectomy.' Kelly grinned, relaxing into the medicine she loved. 'He lived to surf another day.'

Beth grinned back. 'A woman who performs surfboard-ectomies is my kind of doctor. So, do you want the job?'

'Surely you need to check up on me.'

'Matt already did. He phoned your previous bosses this morning. You have glowing credentials from everyone.'

'How did he know who to ask?' Kelly gasped.

'Your son, of course. Apparently Jess thinks it's cool that you'll be working here.'

'Matt asked Jess?'

'He's his uncle, isn't he?'

There was a statement to make her catch her breath. It suggested that Matt had a relationship with Jess that had nothing to do with her. Maybe he did, but…

My home is special and I wish to share it with you.

She couldn't get rid of that stupid statement. Why did the words keep coming back and why did they make her feel edgy? Like the walls were closing in?

She was being paranoid, she decided. She and Jess were accepting Matt's kindness while Jess recuperated. That was all. And it was fine that Jess had told Matt where she'd trained.

And the kiss?

The kiss had been an aberration, she told herself—a momentary temptation and weakness. So why had it felt like a beginning?

'So, do you want the job?' Beth asked brightly again. 'There's a heap of forms to complete if you do. You can take them with you and fill them in while Jess watches his surf videos.'

'How do you know Jess watches surf videos?'

'Matt told me. He took him some sci-fi movies and Jess politely declined. Matt thinks he's a bit obsessed.'

'He told you he thinks Jessie's obsessed?'

'Hey,' Beth said, and held up her hands as if in surrender. 'I'm a mother of three teenagers. I understand obsession. Matt doesn't.'

'But he told you. It's none of his business.'

'Maybe he wants it to be his business,' Beth said mildly. 'But as for me, I'm butting out, right now.'

'So Matt's been lending you sci-fi movies?'

Kelly had made herself wait a whole half-hour before casually asking the question, and Jess didn't look up from the television when she did.

'Yeah. They were dumb. He didn't mind, though, when I refused. It's not like he bought them or anything—they're borrowed. I told him I had more surfing stuff than I could handle but he didn't seem interested. Do you know if he can surf?'

'He can. He's not bad.'

'I guess with Dad for a brother he must know how. A surfing surgeon. That's pretty cool. He was telling me about Dad when he was a kid. Mom, they're saying I can go home tomorrow as long as I come in every morning for physiotherapy. Matt says there's loads of room at his place and he has dogs and I can see the surf. And Beth… she's the doctor in Emergency and she's cool…she has a son who's fourteen and a surf nut but he's teaching himself from videos. She asked if I might have time to talk him through them. She'll bring him out to Matt's.'

Right. All organised. This was good. So why did it feel like the ground was sliding away from under her? Why was she feeling like she was more out of control that she'd ever been?

'That's great,' she managed. 'And I have a job.'

'I know that, too,' Jess said. 'Or I knew they were going to offer. Everyone knows everything around here, even the janitor.' He looked up at her then, with that shy, warm smile that was so like his father's it still did her head in. 'If I had to wipe out, it was pretty lucky I wiped out here. It almost feels like home.'

Home. There was that word again.

She shook off her unease and checked the colour of Jess's toes, not because she needed to—she was sure even a minuscule change wouldn't have escaped Matt's attention. But she needed to be doing something.

She wished she could start work this morning instead of in two days' time when the forms had been cleared. She wished...

She wished she was doing something that wasn't controlled by Matt Eveldene and his hospital and his home.

She wished she wasn't tempted.

There was no way Kelly was raiding Matt's refrigerator again. She and Jess would be independent. So after leaving the hospital she headed to the supermarket Matt had taken her to that first night he'd taken her to his place.

After stocking up on provisions, she made for home. No, she corrected herself, she made for *Matt's place*. Why the differentiation was important she didn't know, but it was. She did Jess's washing then, looking for something else to do, she took the dogs for a walk on the beach.

She wished Jess wasn't so fiercely independent. If he was younger and less fierce about his boundaries she could go back to the hospital and talk to him or read, or even help while he did his physio.

If Matt offered, would Jess let him help?

'The kid needs a father.' Various people had said that to her over the years, or variations on the theme. 'How does he cope without a father figure?'

He'd coped fine. She was proud of him.

So why was she stalking along the beach like she was angry? Was she angry?

If the Eveldenes had been supportive all those years ago, if they'd offered a home and family to her and her son, would she have wanted it?

Did she want it now?

She wasn't making sense, even to herself.

Disconcerted, she headed back to the house. She felt aimless, totally disoriented.

She could surf, but for once there was no one surfing at the far headlands and one of her rules was not surfing without other surfers in sight. She'd made that rule up for Jess. As a kid she'd surfed whenever she'd wanted, but becoming a mother had changed the ground rules. Tempting as it was, if she surfed alone then Jess would, too.

She needed to ask Matt not to, she decided. There was already a hint of change of allegiance in Jess's attitude. She could hear him in her imagination.

'If Matt surfs alone, I don't see why you're worried.'

Oh, for heaven's sake, get over yourself, she told herself. She was worrying about shadows. She turned her back on the ocean and headed for her little kitchen. What to do? What to do?

Bake?

She never baked. She didn't even cook much. In their shoebox of an apartment in Hawaii she had a two-ring burner and a microwave.

'If this place is "home" then I might as well pretend it really is,' she told herself. 'And what do normal people do at home? Bake.'

So she would. She'd make a welcome-home cake for Jess. How hard could it be?

'I'll need a pinafore,' she told the dogs, egging herself

into the role of cook-extraordinaire. 'And maybe some fluffy slippers and hair curlers.'

The dogs wagged their tails, bemused, as well they might be. Kelly cooking? Kelly was a bit bemused herself.

Matt climbed out of the car, taking a breath of the sea air to ground himself—and smelled burning. Smoke was wafting from the windows at the end of the house. He ran, grabbing his phone so he could call emergency services, imagining the worst.

It wasn't the worst. Kelly was at her kitchen bench, surrounded by smoke, staring mournfully at something that looked like a withered, black pyramid.

She looked totally, absolutely crestfallen.

The pyramid was oozing the smoke. It smelled of burned citrus. It was surrounded by flour, eggshells, milk cartons, cream cartons, splattered...mess. The dogs were cruising, obviously hoovering up a week's worth of treats in one hit. Bess was doing better than Spike because she could reach higher. Whatever had splattered had hit walls as well as floor.

'I think I know what the problem is,' Kelly said mournfully, not taking her eyes from the pyramid. 'I should have put the orange syrup on after it was cooked, not before. It sort of spilled over the sides and the bottom of the oven started to smoke. And then flame. And it cooked so fast...'

She had mixture on her face, through her hair, on her jeans and T-shirt. She looked...

Delicious.

'Argument with the mixer?' he ventured, trying desperately not to laugh, and she glared at the offending object as if it was totally to blame.

'I wanted to check if it was thick enough. I lifted the beaters for a second. And your oven's faulty. The recipe said three-fifty degrees for three-quarters of an hour and your oven only goes to two hundred and eighty. But look what it did after fifteen minutes?'

He couldn't help it. His mouth twitched.

'Don't you dare laugh.'

'No,' he said, and walked—or rather squelched—to the bench. She had her laptop sitting on the fruit bowl, where it had, luckily, been shielded from the mixer by fruit.

He read the screen. Yep, the instructions read three-fifty degrees for forty minutes. But this was an American site. An American recipe.

'You ever heard of Celsius versus Fahrenheit?' he asked.

She stared at him, her eyes widening in dawning horror. 'Celsius…'

'And we drive on the left side of the road, too,' he said apologetically. 'Whoops.'

'Celsius! That'd be…' She did a quick calculation in her head. 'A hundred and seventy. Oh, my… Why didn't they say?'

'Because *they're* American.'

'That's crazy.'

'Americans *are* crazy. Almost the whole world—apart from Americans—uses Celsius.'

'Now you're insulting my country as well as my cooking.'

He grinned, took a dollop of goop from the bench and tasted. 'I'm not insulting your cooking. This is good. Ganache?'

She peered suspiciously at the recipe and checked. 'Yes,' she conceded.

'Did you try and layer it into the cake before you cooked it?'

She glowered. 'I'm not completely dumb. It's still in the bowl. Or at least,' she corrected, 'most of it's still in the bowl.'

'So…' He went back to the recipe, fascinated. 'We have

Grand Marnier ganache, some of it still in the bowl, plus chocolate orange cake, slightly singed.'

'Stupid recipe,' she muttered. 'If I can track neural pathways and get high distinctions for forensic pathology, I should be able to follow basic instructions. But no. And now you're making things worse by being supercilious. Go away. Do something useful, like look up cake shop addresses online.'

'You want a welcome-home cake for Jess?'

'That's the idea.'

'I can cook.'

'Right.'

'Honest.' He folded his arms and surveyed cook and kitchen with glinting amusement. She was cute, he thought. She was really cute. And with ganache on her nose he had a strong desire to...

Um...his thoughts had better change direction fast.

'We still have heaps of ganache,' he said. 'We could try again.'

'Again? Are you out of your mind? Your oven needs a jackhammer. I might need to buy you another one.'

He opened the oven. Orange syrup, baked on hard...

He rolled up his sleeves. 'This is men's work,' he said, feeling the need to beat his chest a little. 'Nothing to it.'

'You're lying.'

'I'll prove it. You scrub the walls, I'll scrub the oven.'

'I'd rather fence off the whole area and let it moulder.'

'What would you do if you did this at home?' he demanded, startled.

'Move. We only ever rent.'

He looked at her with incredulity. 'I can't imagine how you get references.'

'I'm a good tenant,' she said with dignity. 'I just don't rent ovens. Apartments with ovens cost more and now I see why. They're lethal.'

'They're fun.'

'Says the man who's offering to scrub one? Matt, it's okay. I made this mess. I'll clean it up.'

'You won't,' he said, suddenly serious. 'I've left you to face enough messes on your own. The least I can do is help you with this one.'

He wouldn't take no for an answer. He changed into jeans and T-shirt and locked the dogs outside, then for half an hour they scrubbed and cleaned. She grew more and more mortified. Then, the last wall wiped, the last pot cleaned, he hauled ingredients and pots and bowls out again and she forgot about being embarrassed, regarding him with horror.

'Matt, this recipe is lethal.'

'This recipe looks great.'

'It could have killed me. I could be a smouldering pile of ash on top of what remains of your glorious home right now.'

'Let's not get carried away.'

'It has it in for me.'

'You just lack the necessary qualification. Did I tell you I'm a surgeon? Precision is my byword. You want to be second in command?'

'No,' she said. 'Think of me as the janitor. Washing up's my forte.'

'I need an assistant,' he said. 'As of now you're employed by Gold Coast Central. As senior surgeon I have the right to tell junior staff what to do. I want two fifty grams of plain flour measured out into a bowl. The scales are in metric. Don't you dare think about conversion. Get to it now, Dr Eveldene. Flour. Weigh. Stat!'

And there was nothing else for a woman to do. Flour. Weigh. Stat.

* * *

This man was a surgeon and that was how he approached his cooking. He treated it as a tricky piece of surgery, like reconstructing a child's knee, with meticulous attention given to detail at every stage.

He insisted on scrupulous cleanliness. Measurements had to be correct almost to the closest gram. Tins were to be lined with perfect circles of baking paper—when her circles were a bit wobbly he made her cut more. Instructions were read aloud by his 'assistant' then checked by Matt, then rechecked as soon as the procedure was complete. There was not a sliver of room for error. And pity any recipe writer who got it wrong, because Kelly could hardly imagine what Matt's reaction would be if he didn't get it right first time.

But, of course, he did. An hour and a half later they were sitting at the kitchen table, admiring a cake that looked better than the picture on the internet. All they had to do when Jess arrived was slice it and insert the ganache.

'And I'll do that,' Matt said sternly.

'You're the surgeon,' she admitted. They were eating toasted sandwiches, which Matt had kindly allowed her to make—under supervision. She grinned. 'There's no need to keep looking at it. I can only cope with so much smugness before I crack and put the ganache where it really oughtn't to be put.'

'It's hard not to be smug about perfection.' He looked even more smug and she lifted the ganache bowl. He grinned back at her and held his hands up in surrender. 'Hey, I'm not being smug about *my* work. I'm being smug about *our* work.'

'Very generous. When did you learn to cook?'

'When I was a kid. We had a cook-housekeeper. Mrs Marsh. Jess used to escape to the surf, but while I was too young to go with him, the kitchen was my refuge.'

'Your childhood was tough, huh?'

'Poor little rich kids,' he said dryly. 'It was better for me than for Jess. He was the elder so he was expected to take over the business. The pressure on him was enormous but I learned to stay out of the way.' He hesitated. 'When I was really young I'd try and intervene. I remember screaming at my father, "*Leave my Jess alone*." I was belted for my pains and Jess told me he'd do the same to me if I ever tried to interfere again. Not that he would. But I learned…the only way was to disappear.'

'It's a wonder you're still in Australia.'

'Once I got my medical degree I had some form of protection.' He hesitated. 'Even that was down to Jess, though. When I was due to start university my father was so angry with Jess he hardly noticed what I was doing. Jess was the oldest, Jess had to pull himself together and take over what was expected of him. While I was at university he thought I was still under control. I put my head down and kept out of his way. That feels bad now. I should have deflected more of his anger.'

'I think there's been enough guilt,' Kelly told him. 'Jess would have hated you to carry more.'

'He would have wanted me to care for you.'

'I didn't need to be cared for,' she said with some asperity. 'Or maybe I did, but Jess did enough. He married me, he settled my future and he knew I had the strength to take his legacy forward.'

'He knew how strong you were,' Matt said, and lifted his hand and touched her face, a whisper of a touch, tracing her cheekbones and sending all sorts of weird currents through her body, and not one of them bad. 'His independent Kelly.'

If he kept touching her… If she just leaned forward…

'I feel like a surf,' she said, pushing her plate away, striving desperately to push away the longings this man was starting to engender. 'We have an hour before dark. Would you like...?'

'I would like,' he said gravely, and his eyes didn't leave hers. 'I would like very much.'

There was only so much temptation a woman could resist.

They surfed as they'd surfed that morning, but things had changed. They lay out on the sunset-tinged waves, waiting for the next wave to carry them in, but tonight, by unspoken mutual consent, they caught the same waves. And there was no fancy surfing from Kelly. Even though she had the zippy short board, even though her board would have let her run rings around Matt, she was content to ride the force into the shallows beside Matt.

Over and over they caught the waves, but there was no speaking. There seemed no need. It seemed all the talking had been done, everything they needed to know had been discovered, and what was before them now was predestined.

The sun sank low over the hills, sending fire out over the waves. The moon rose over the sea, hanging low, promising ribbons of silver when the sun's rays stopped competing for air play.

Night. The rays would come in to feed. Visibility was dropping by the second. It was time to leave.

They rode the last wave to the beach, tugged the boards up past the high-water mark and left them there. Matt took her hand and led her up to the house and still no words needed to be spoken.

This is right, Kelly thought, a great wash of peace settling over her as her body tingled with anticipation of what was to come.

That was a dumb thought. It was a thought that had to be shelved, and it was, because how could she think of anything but Matt as he led her into the shower off his bedroom? Matt, as he stepped into the shower with her...?

She couldn't think past his body. The rippling muscles of his chest, the traces of sand in the hollows at his shoulders, the way the water ran from his smile right down to his feet. She could see every long, gorgeous inch of him. The water from the shower ran over them, and for this night, for now, every single thing in the world could be forgotten except that this was Matt and he was here, now, and for tonight he was hers.

Nothing else could matter.

'You know this is not a one-night stand,' he muttered thickly into her hair as they stood under the warm water, as somehow their costumes disappeared, as somehow their bodies seemed to be merging into each other.

Not a one-night stand. What was he saying?

It didn't matter, though, because she wasn't thinking past right now, this minute, as Matt flicked off the shower, grabbed towels and started, deliciously, to dry her. This minute, as Matt hung the towels—okay, she did allow herself a moment to be distracted here and think that even now the man was house-proud—but she didn't allow herself to be distracted for more than a millisecond.

Because Matt was lifting her, holding her hard and tight against his body, skin against skin, and it was the most erotic sensation in the world.

And Matt was carrying her back to the bedroom, setting her down on crisp, cool sheets, gazing down at her, taking in every inch of her as she was doing right back to him.

And finally he came down to her. Finally he gathered her into his arms and he made her feel as she'd never felt in her life before.

He made her feel as if she'd found her home.

CHAPTER EIGHT

MATT TOOK A couple of hours off work the next day so he could help bring Jess home. Jess lay with his leg stretched out in the back seat of Matt's car and he signalled his approval as soon as they turned into the main gates.

'Neat place.'

His approval grew even stronger when he saw his room, the veranda—and Matt's indulgent, toys-for-boys media room.

'Can we stay here for ever?' he demanded, and Matt quirked a brow at Kelly and Kelly blushed from the toes up. Why? What was wrong with her?

She knew exactly what was wrong with her.

She'd been tempted and she'd caved right in.

Matt had organised decent crutches, which made Jess pretty much independent. The bathroom in their apartment had obviously been built with Matt's mother in mind. Its easy access and built-in seat catered for the needs of an elderly woman now and in the future, so it was perfect for Jess. Jess checked it out and was obliged to use his approval rating's highest score.

'Über-neat. Now I don't need anyone fussing.'

'Certainly not me,' Kelly agreed, and went and made them all sandwiches. She could at least make sandwiches, she thought ruefully. She wasn't completely useless.

But, then…last night's cake disaster had turned into a success.

Define success?

Success was a highly edible, orange ganache gateau, she told herself, carrying the amazing creation out to the veranda where they'd settled. Nothing else.

'Wow,' Jess said, eyes wide. 'Where did that come from?'

'Your mother made it,' Matt said with aplomb, and Jess looked at him as if he'd lost his mind.

'Not in a million years. Mom struggles with hamburgers.'

'I do not,' Kelly said hotly. 'Or at least, not very much.'

Both guys grinned. Identical smiles.

It did something to her heart. It made her feel…

'You cut,' Matt said, handing her the knife, and she shook her head.

'You're the surgeon.'

'And you're the mother,' Matt said softly. 'You're the mother welcoming her kid home.'

Matt went back to work. Jess went to sleep. Kelly took a book and she and the dogs headed for the beach.

She couldn't read. She walked the dogs but it didn't help. Even a swim couldn't clear her head.

What was happening was some strange, sweet siren song. Temptation plus. Come home… Come home…

What was wrong with it? Why was she so nervous?

Matt was gorgeous. She was pretty sure he wasn't making love to her out of pity or some weird misguided attachment to his long-dead brother. She was pretty sure he'd stopped seeing her as Jess's widow, as she'd stopped looking at him as Jess's brother. He was just…Matt. The past was forgotten, or maybe not forgotten but so far in the past that it was simply a shadow that could be tucked away and left to lie in peace.

Last night had been awesome, and today... The way he'd kissed her before he'd left for the hospital this morning... The way he'd looked at her as she and Jess had laughed over their cake... There was the promise of more. Much, much more.

Home.

See, that was the problem. That was what was making her nervous.

Home.

Matt had outpatients all afternoon. This was the day of the week he liked best. It was his day when patients came for their final check-up after major surgery.

He saw sixty-year-old Lily Devett who'd fallen over her cat and broken her arm. Yes, it had been a nasty fracture but the bones hadn't splintered or broken the skin. Pinning the bones together had been relatively easy.

She brought in chocolate cookies, a bottle of truly excellent whisky and gave him a hug that almost squeezed the breath out of him. 'I can't believe how good it is. When I broke it I thought that's it, it's a downhill road to the nursing home, but it's as good as new. I can even carry my cat again.'

'Just don't fall over it again.' He smiled, and moved on to see Doug Lamworth.

Doug was fifty-two and had tripped while playing a tricky golf shot. The ball had landed on the other side of a creek, the ground was rough and unstable but Doug had refused to play a drop shot. He'd fallen and ended up with an appalling hip injury. It had taken Matt tense, difficult hours in surgery to ensure Doug wouldn't walk with a limp for the rest of his life, but his gratitude wasn't forthcoming.

'It still aches,' Doug snapped. 'After six weeks you'd

think it'd be right. I don't know what you fellas did in there but you've mucked me round worse than the fall. The bruises…hell. And now your blasted registrar won't give me any more of that codeine stuff. I need it. I tell you, I've just about had enough.'

He left without a script for more of the highly addictive drug, complaining he didn't have time for the physiotherapy Matt told him would work much better than painkillers. He left promising he'd sue the pants off Matt if he wasn't better by the time he and his mates left for their Thailand holiday, and telling him that, by the way, he needed a certificate to try and get a compassionate upgrade to business class.

He left and Matt found himself grinning. He thought he'd enjoy telling Kelly about it tonight.

Telling Kelly… There was a thought. Going home tonight and finding Kelly waiting for him.

And suddenly he found himself thinking of his ex-wife. He'd loved coming home and finding her there. He'd loved the concept of wife and family. It was just that Jenny hadn't wanted to fit in. She'd wanted another sort of life and he'd never really understood what.

Was this his second chance?

Things were better. Things had changed since Jenny.

He knew now that things would never have worked out between him and Jenny. They'd been incompatible, and the thought gave him pause. How could things be different with Kelly? One night's passion wouldn't make a long-term commitment.

But the way she'd felt… The way her body had responded to his… It had felt more than right. It had felt as if he'd been waiting all his life to find her.

His next patient was Herman Briggs, who had a list of complaints a mile long. Apparently his knee replacement should have cured all his ills. At Matt's insistence he'd lost

weight before the operation but he'd put it back on with
interest. Now his hip was playing up, he had a sore back
and his other knee was hurting. What was Matt going to
do about it?

Matt organised X-rays, sent him back to the dietician
and looked forward to going home to Kelly.

She wasn't sure of the rules.

'Why are you pacing?' Jess demanded. He'd abandoned
his video game, distracted by his mother's distraction. 'Is
there a problem?'

'I'm not pacing.'

'You look like you're pacing.'

'I'm waiting for Matt.'

'Why?'

The question brought her up short. She turned from the
window and stared at her son.

Jess was stretched out on the settee. His gaming con-
sole was linked to the television. He'd been using a remote to control cartoon characters doing surf stunts. He
looked content.

Jess. Her lovely, placid Jess who took what came, who'd
been her life for so long.

Why was she pacing?

There'd been illnesses and injuries before, of course
there had. This might be an upmarket place to find themselves in while he recovered but essentially things were
the same. Jess got on with his life, she got on with hers,
but they were there for each other.

She was his mom. Today was Jess's first day home
from hospital. It was well after seven and she hadn't even
thought about dinner.

Why? Because she was waiting for Matt?

She was thinking about Matt rather than thinking about
her son.

And suddenly she felt like she'd been hit by ice-cold water.

Was she nuts? She'd just met a man again whom she'd thought a toe-rag for years. She'd changed her mind. More than that, she'd fallen in lust for him and now she was mooning about, waiting for him like a lovesick teenager.

Or the little wife. When he got home would she invite him in, cook for all of them, start being a family?

It's a wonder she wasn't standing by the door, slippers in one hand, pipe in the other.

The vision was so ridiculous that she chuckled and Jess looked at her curiously. 'What's the joke?'

'Me being dumb.'

'You're dumb all the time. What makes now something to laugh over?'

She grimaced, grabbed a cushion and tossed it at him. 'Dinner?'

'Yes,' Jess said cautiously. He knew her cooking skills and this seemed a place where take-out seemed unlikely.

'Hamburgers,' she said, and he relaxed.

'Yay.'

She headed for the apartment kitchenette and thought that from tonight she needed to step back. To slow down and think of Jess first.

She needed to close the dividing wall between the apartments until she'd settled her hormones into some sort of sensible, working order.

Matt got home at eight and the apartment side of his house was lit. His side of the house was in darkness.

The dogs came to greet him as he garaged the car but they weren't there instantly, as they normally were. He stooped to pat them and their coats were warm, as if they'd just emerged from somewhere cosy.

He looked at the apartment windows, and then looked at his.

Separate houses?

Kelly emerged onto the veranda and walked along to meet him.

'Hey,' he said, and reached for her. She let him hug her, she responded to his kiss, sinking into him, but only briefly and the kiss was less than quarter baked before she tugged away.

'Um…Matt, no.'

'No?'

'Jess's home.'

'Right.' He wasn't sure how to take that. 'So that means…'

'It means we need to step back,' she said, slightly un-evenly, as if the kiss had unsettled her—as well it might. It had sure unsettled him. He had an urgent desire to lift her up and carry her into his den, caveman style. He wanted, quite desperately, to have his wicked way with her—and let her have her wicked way with him.

But there was no humour in her eyes, and the passion of the morning had been subdued.

'Jess has known you less than a week,' she told him. 'He hardly knows you.'

'Is that another way of saying you hardly know me?'

'I guess it is,' she whispered. 'Matt, you're my husband's brother. I don't know why I'm responding to you like I am and I need time to figure it out.'

'You don't want to figure it out together?'

'But where does that leave Jess?' she asked. 'He's smart. He has eyes in the back of his head where I'm concerned. He knows I'm conflicted about seeing you again, even though he knows very little about our history. So now he needs to get to know you—as his uncle. I'm not throwing his mother's lover into the equation.'

'Kelly…'

'It won't hurt,' she said, but he knew it did. Her voice wobbled a bit and he thought that for all her planning she was still unsure. Still tempted. 'It can't hurt to step back a bit.'

Wrong. It hurt a lot. The hunger inside him was primitive. He wanted this woman and he wanted her now, but she was making sense.

She was right. His brother's son was just through the wall. There were complications.

And in the middle of these complications…one man and one woman who wanted each other.

'Give us time, Matt,' Kelly pleaded. 'Let things settle. Let Jess get to know you—as his uncle.'

He didn't want it to make sense, but it did.

'Not…after he goes to bed?' he said without much hope, and she snorted.

'Um…we're talking seventeen-year-old with friends on the other side of the world,' she said. 'Teenage sleeping habits. You want me to try tucking him into bed at nine and sending him to sleep with a bedtime story?'

'A really boring bedtime story?' he suggested without much hope, but at least her smile was back. She chuckled.

'Yeah? Like that'll work. He'll be checking tweets over my sleeping body.'

'That's my plans shot,' he said morosely, and she chuckled.

'Not for ever,' she said lightly. 'We just need to take our time.'

'I'll slope off and take a cold shower, then.'

'Come over and have leftover hamburgers with Jess afterwards.'

'I have the makings of steak and peppercorn sauce.'

'See, there's the divide between us,' she told him. 'Unless you've bought your peppercorn sauce in a bottle, we have a chasm a mile wide.'

'We can bridge it.'

'We might,' she said, and stood on tiptoe and kissed him lightly on the cheek, then stepped back fast before he could respond. 'But it'll take time, and both of us need to be patient.'

He showered. He cooked and ate his steak—with his sauce that didn't come out of a bottle. Then he wandered along the veranda. The French doors of Kelly's apartment were wide open, and he could hear the sound of waves crashing inside.

Waves. Inside. Huh?

He didn't need to knock or call out because the dogs had been by Jessie's side by the settee. They bounded across to him as they sensed his presence.

Kelly was curled in an armchair, reading. Jess was sprawled on the settee, controlling surfers on the television. Waves. Lots of waves.

He put down the remote and grinned. 'Hey, Matt.'

Would it be easier or harder if he was less like his brother? Matt wondered. The way his heart twisted...

'Hey, yourself,' he said, as Kelly looked up and smiled and his heart did a little more twisting. 'You guys look comfortable,' he managed.

'We're good at making transitory places home,' Kelly told him, and he looked at the scattered jumble of teenage detritus, the piles of obviously to-be-read books and comics on the table, the bunch of wildflowers popped randomly into a tall drinking glass, already starting to drop petals.

'You look like you want to tidy us up,' Kelly said, and he caught himself. That was dumb. He'd just been...looking.

'It's your apartment for the duration. You're welcome to do what you want with it.'

'Thank you,' Kelly said, and put her book aside. 'It will be neat when we leave. We were about to have hot chocolate. You want some?'

'I… Thank you.'

'My pleasure.' She headed for the kitchenette while Jess lay back on the settee and regarded him with eyes that were curiously assessing. How much could the kid guess about what had gone on with his mother?

'Neat freak, huh?' he asked, but his tone was friendly.

'I guess I have to be. Non-neat surgeons tend to do things like leave swabs inside people.'

'So no swabs in me?'

'Not a snowball's chance in a bushfire. Can I check your leg?'

They both relaxed at that. Doctor-patient was a relationship they both understood. They knew where they were.

And the examination was even more reassuring. Jess was healing with the resilience of the young. His leg looked better than Matt had hoped, and he set the blanket back over it, feeling good.

'So when's the soonest I can surf again?' Jess asked, and the question oddly threw him. Suddenly he no longer felt good.

Memories of his brother were surfacing. 'When can I surf?' The words had been a constant in his childhood, a desperate plea. Surfing had been an escape for Jess, but for the much younger Matt Jess's surfing had meant long days alone with a seething father and a mother who'd suffered because of his father's anger.

It wasn't surfing's fault. Matt had found his own ways of escape, but for Jess surfing had become an obsession. He looked down at his brother's son, and he saw evidence of the same.

Surfing was an obsession for this kid, too.

'In three months you can cope with gentle surf and no

tricks,' he told him, struggling to rid himself of shadows. 'But you need to wait for six months for the big-boy stuff. If you get hit again before your leg's completely healed, you risk lifetime damage.'

'Six months *is* a lifetime,' Jess groaned.

'You could always do something useful in the meantime.'

There was a sudden stillness in the room. Kelly had been stirring the hot chocolate. The stirring stopped.

'Like what?' Jess said. His face had gone blank.

So had Kelly's.

Step back, Matt told himself. This was none of his business.

But, then, he was this kid's uncle. Who else did this boy have looking out for him except a mother who was clearly surf mad herself?

What better time to present an alternative than when Jess was looking at an enforced six-month break? Did he intend spending the whole six months playing computer games? Staring out the window at distant surfers, aching to join them?

'I did suggest you might go to school here,' he said diffidently. 'Make some friends. Maybe even pick up a few subjects that might be useful for later.'

'Later when?'

'When you're old enough not to want to spend every minute surfing.'

There was another silence, even more loaded this time. Jess suddenly looked mutinous. 'Mom and I have a deal.'

'What sort of deal?'

'I'll surf and she keeps off my back about anything else.'

What sort of a deal was that? 'It seems a bit one-sided to me,' he said mildly.

'Yeah, and Mom says my grandfather hated surfing, too,' Jess snapped.

'I don't hate surfing.'

'You want me to do calculus and history instead?'

'It's not my business.'

'It's not, is it?' Kelly said from the kitchenette, and she set down the mugs she'd been about to carry across to them. 'What Jess and I do is for us to decide. Matt, we're incredibly grateful for the use of this apartment but if you're about to try forcing Jess back to school then the deal's off. We'll manage without.'

'I'm not forcing anyone anywhere.'

'Good,' she snapped. 'Your family's done enough damage as it is.'

What followed was another one of those loaded silences, but it was worse this time. 'I'm not my father,' he said at last, because it was all he could think of to say.

'No,' she said. 'And as far as I know, uncles have no jurisdiction over their nephews.'

'They don't. I'm sorry.'

'Will you be judgmental about Jess's surfing the whole time we're here?'

'Of course not.' He raked his hair in exasperation. How to mess with a relationship in two short minutes.

'I don't need school,' Jess growled. 'I've done enough study.'

The kid was seventeen! 'For ever?'

'This is none of your business,' Kelly snapped. 'Do you want a hot chocolate or not?'

She lifted the chocolate and he wasn't sure where she was offering to send it. As an air-based missile?

'I seem to have put my foot in it.'

'You have,' she said cordially. 'Jess and I do things our way and we don't take kindly to interference from the Eveldenes.'

'My family has hardly interfered.'

'They haven't, have they?'

'You sound like you resent that.'

'I contacted your father when your brother was ill,' she said, and every trace of warmth was suddenly gone. 'You have no idea how hard that was, for a seventeen-year-old to find the courage to phone the great Henry Eveldene. I thought if we had a little money I could persuade Jess to see a psychiatrist. But you know what your father said? "I'm not sending money to that waste of space. Tell him to give up surfing and come home." That's it. And now here you are...'

'I'm not withdrawing help because Jess wants to surf.'

'No,' she said flatly. 'And for that we're grateful. But Jess doesn't need to go to school.'

He was going about this all the wrong way. He raked his hair again, exasperated. They were living in their own little world, these two. Sure, Kelly had been hurt by his family, but did that allow her to be a negligent parent? Encouraging her son not to go to school?

'You hurt your leg,' he told Jess, struggling to keep things on an even keel. 'It seems this time you've been lucky and you'll get back to surfing. But eventually you'll want security, a home.' He gestured around him to the house he'd built with such care, the house that had become his refuge. 'Somewhere like this. You won't earn this from surfing.'

'Does it matter?' Kelly demanded. 'That we don't have a home?'

'Of course it matters. Look at the mess you're in now.'

'We're not in a mess,' she snapped. 'We're independent. We don't need anyone and we can handle our issues ourselves. Our only problem now is that we seem to have a judgmental landlord. That doesn't matter. We've coped with landlords before. If they're bad we move on.'

'Hey, don't threaten that yet,' Jess said, startled. 'Mom,

he's being a stuffed shirt, that doesn't mean we need to move. This place is ace. We can manage a bit of aggro.'

'I'm not being aggressive!'

'Nah,' Jess said thoughtfully. 'But pushy. I'd have thought Dad's brother might be more laid-back. Mom, cut him some slack. Matt, have a drink and move on. I want to stay here.'

'I'd like to stay here, too,' Kelly said. 'But not if Matt's controlling. Not if he intends to bully you.'

'I'm not bullying,' Matt snapped. 'And I'll back off. But I'll have a drink next door, thank you.'

'Are you taking your bat and ball and going home?' she demanded. 'Just because we won't let you be like your father?'

'I am not like my father!' His words were an explosion, and even the dogs responded. Spike even whimpered and headed under Jessie's rug. What a traitor!

'Of course you're not,' Jess said at last, as the echoes died. 'Have a hot chocolate and forget about it.'

'I need to sleep. I have work tomorrow.'

'Bat and ball,' Kelly snapped, and he glared, clicked his fingers at the dogs and headed for the door.

The dogs didn't follow. He reached the veranda and looked back. Every single one of them was looking at him with reproach—even the dogs.

Jess went back to his computer game. Kelly went into her own room, lay on the bed and stared at the ceiling. She'd have liked to walk on the beach but there was no way she was risking meeting Matt again.

They should leave. If Matt intended to even think about controlling Jess… He mustn't.

She'd been so careful, for all her son's life. Her Jess adored surfing. She knew what it meant to him, so she'd worked her life and his around it. She'd had to. She'd seen what denying that passion had done to his father. So far Jess had shown no signs of his father's depression and that was the way it was staying.

Even if it meant walking away from Matt Eveldene?

Even that. Of course that. If he put one more step wrong... If he tried to control...

Even if she wanted him?

'And that's something you need to forget about,' she told the ceiling. 'Temptation is just plain stupid. From now on, you go back to being a mom. You go back to protecting Jess, no matter what the cost.'

CHAPTER NINE

HE WAS THEIR landlord. They were his tenants. From that night on, that was the way things needed to operate. He'd keep out of their lives. What he said or thought was none of their business, and vice versa.

Luckily, things were frantic at work. King tides meant the surf was huge. Every novice surfer in the country seemed to be daring themselves past their limit—and ending up in Gold Coast Central. Almost all the injuries were orthopaedic. Matt was needed full time.

He stopped surfing in the mornings. He walked his dogs at dawn and then left for the hospital before there was any movement next door. He did his paperwork in his office instead of taking it home. Normally he wouldn't—it wasn't fair on the dogs—but the dogs seemed to be having a fine time with Jess. When he did get home they bounded out to meet him, but they were always toasty warm and he knew where they'd been.

'Are you avoiding us?' He got home one night and Jess was on the veranda settee, watching the sunset surfers with fieldglasses.

'Just busy,' he said briefly. 'You have a follow-up appointment in two days. I'll see you then.'

'It seems dumb only to see you at the hospital.'

It did.

'I crossed a line,' he said. 'I thought I should back off.'

'Just don't cross the line again,' Jess said cheerfully. 'You make Mom mad. We have doughnuts. You want to come in and have supper?'

'Does your mother want me to?'

'Mom's got her knickers in a twist about you. She needs to get over it.'

'Well, when she gets over it, I'll join you.'

'She's being weird.'

'Then it's best we leave it,' Matt told him. 'We wouldn't want to upset your mother.'

Only he did want to upset Jess's mother. Or something. It nearly killed him to have things hanging in limbo. Each day that passed it seemed worse, like there was tension hanging over his home and his hospital.

Kelly, on the other hand, seemed remarkably unperturbed.

'She's a great doctor,' Beth told him. 'The best. Kids are brought into Emergency and she manages to get the priorities sorted and reassure everyone at the same time. Kids relax with her. We had a boy come in yesterday with concussion and a broken collar bone. He was in pain and his mother was hysterical. The kid had fallen through a roof he'd been forbidden to climb and his mum was so out of it she was saying, "I'll kill him, I'll kill him." Kelly had them sorted in minutes. "Don't you just hate it when they scare you like this?" she said to the mum. "But no killing, not yet. Let me patch him up and then he's all yours." The woman finally ended up giggling. She got the kid smiling, too. Can we keep her?'

'She's only here until her own kid gets better.'

'Then put on a heavier cast and prescribe twelve months of Australian physiotherapy. Keep her. She's good.'

He had an irrational urge to see for himself. The orthopaedic department was too far from Emergency and for the first time in years he found himself wishing he could change specialties. But he was occasionally needed there. Later that morning Beth called him to assess X-rays of a guy who'd come off a motorbike. He was about to leave when noise at the entrance caught his attention.

Paramedics had brought in a child, barely more than a toddler, and Matt saw at once what the problem was. She had her big toe stuck in a bath outlet. The pipe had been cut and she'd been brought in with the pipe still attached.

The noise was deafening. The little girl was hysterical with fear and pain. Her sobbing mother could hardly be prised away, and her father was shouting random commands at the top of his lungs. 'Elly, keep still. Get the thing off. How much longer? I thought you called yourself a hospital. I'll call the fire department, they'll be more use.'

Kelly had obviously once again been paired with Emma, and Emma was struggling to make herself heard. Kelly was struggling to get past the mother and assess the situation. She was attempting to calm the little one, while Emma was trying to hold the irate father back. 'Please, if you could leave her to us…'

The paramedics weren't helping. The situation was escalating.

Was it time for an orthopaedic surgeon to step in, even if it wasn't his patch?

'What's the child's name?' he asked the closest paramedic.

'Elly Woodman, aged two. They've all been screaming since we reached them but we need to go. We have a coronary call waiting.'

'Her parents' names?'

'Sarah and Ben Woodman. The dad's a lawyer and he's already threatening to sue. Good luck, mate.'

The paramedics left. Kelly glanced up, saw him and sent him a silent plea.

There was nothing for it. Matt took a deep breath and dived right in.

'Mr Woodman.' His deep growl cut across the commotion like a harsh blow. He aimed himself directly at the little girl's father, no one else.

'There are too many people in here,' Matt said, fixing his gaze on the young lawyer. 'We need to settle your daughter so we can give her an anaesthetic, but we need space. Therefore her mother stays and that's all. Dr Kellerman—Emma—will take you to Administration, where you can fill in admission details. Please leave.'

'But I'm supposed to be—' Emma ventured, but Matt cut her off with a placatory glance.

'I'm taking over assisting Dr Eveldene.' He laid a hand on the mother's shoulder. 'Stop crying,' he said, and it was a command, not a plea. 'You're scaring your daughter.'

'I can't...' the woman sobbed.

'Stop crying or leave with your husband. Your daughter needs you to be a sensible woman, not a watering can. Hold Elly's arm, Doctor,' he ordered Kelly, but Kelly was already moving.

Matt's commands had distracted the child enough for Kelly to take hold. She manoeuvred Elly before her mother could hug her close again. Before the little girl had time to react, Matt took her arm and held it.

They worked as a team, almost instinctively. Kelly swabbed fast while Matt held. She lifted the anaesthetic syringe from the tray and administered it. The syringe was out of sight before the child knew what had happened.

Kelly relaxed. A hysterical child was a nightmare. The thrashing had been making her foot swell even more and the metal groove of the plug was digging in deeper. The department had been stretched to the limit, there'd been no nurses available and coping with only the inexperienced Emma had been impossible.

But Matt's intervention had the situation under immediate control. The fast-acting injection of relaxant and pain-killer took effect almost instantly. Already the little girl was slumping back in her mother's arms.

Emma had successfully steered the lawyer dad away. There was now only the four of them, and as Elly stopped struggling, her mother relaxed.

'I'm…I'm sorry,' she whispered.

'There's no need to be sorry,' Kelly told her, making her voice deliberately soothing. The time for snapping orders was over. 'But now Elly's nice and sleepy we need to move. How do you suggest we go about this, Dr Eveldene?'

'I'm thinking Elly needs a good sleep while we assess the situation. Sarah, keep cuddling Elly,' Matt told the mum. 'We'll elevate her foot to relieve the swelling but we won't do anything until she's totally relaxed. Meanwhile, we'll cover you with blankets so we can make this as cosy as possible. A bit of storytelling might be called for, all about a bear who gets his toe stuck. You can tell her all about the handsome doctor who slips it off while she's asleep.'

'Handsome?' Kelly queried.

'I like incorporating fact with fiction.' Matt grinned and the young mother gave a wobbly smile and things were suddenly okay.

More than okay.

'You're both Dr Eveldenes?' the young woman asked, looking from Kelly's lanyard to Matt's and back again. She'd relaxed now as Elly snuggled peacefully against her. 'Are you married?'

'Um…no,' said Kelly.

'They just live together.' Beth had come in behind them, obviously wanting to check that things were okay. 'They share a house and a name. They have a kid and two dogs so I don't know why they don't just get married and be done with it.'

Whew.

Despite his shock, Matt understood why Beth had said it. Beth had been in the next cubicle, coping with the guy who'd come off his motorbike. She'd have heard what was happening but not been able to help. Now she was adding her bit, distracting the mother still further. 'There's a spare bed in cubicle five,' she told the young mum. 'It's the quietest. You snuggle down with your little one while these two discuss marriage. There. All problems solved. I do like a happy ending, don't you?'

And she beamed and chuckled and headed off to cope with the next crisis.

Once Elly was deeply asleep things were straightforward.

Elevation and lubrication didn't work but Plan B succeeded. They wound a fine, strong thread down the length of the tiny toe, over and over, with each round of thread placed hard by the next so the toe was enclosed and compressed. Then Kelly managed to manoeuvre an end through the ring. Then they lubricated the thread and gradually started unwinding, using the thread to push the metal forward as they went.

To everyone's relief the toe gradually worked free. Matt gave a grunt of satisfaction—cutting the metal would have been much harder. The thing was done.

Matt patted the kid's head, said his goodbyes and headed back to his work.

It was after her knock-off time. Kelly was free to go.

But not quite. Jess's physio session was running late. The therapist glanced up as Kelly arrived, and waved her away.

'We need an extra half an hour, Dr Eveldene. Jess is doing great.'

Jess was struggling, Kelly could see that, and it was hurting. He was balancing between two standing bars, trying to bear weight.

Kelly knew her son well enough to understand that he wouldn't want her to watch. She waved and left them to it, then headed up to the rooftop cafeteria. She bought a sandwich and headed outdoors to eat it—and Matt was there.

The rooftop was deserted. There was Matt and one table. There were a dozen more tables to choose from.

Don't be pathetic, she told herself, and sat at his.

'If you're about to talk about what sort of flowers you want our bridesmaids to carry, I'm out of here,' Matt said, and she stared at him and then, to her surprise, found herself chuckling.

'Well, it did work,' she conceded. 'It made Sarah focus on gossip instead of what a bad mother she was for letting Elly get her toe stuck. The only problem is it was overheard by half the emergency staff and rumours have probably reached London by now.'

'You need to stop wearing a wedding ring.'

She looked down at the slim band of gold on her finger, very slim, the cheapest wedding ring they had been able to find all those years ago.

'No.'

'You've been faithful to him all these years?'

'You know I haven't,' she said evenly. 'But I still love him.'

'So do I.'

'I think,' she said quietly, hearing his pain, 'that your loss must have been as great or even greater than mine. I was able to mourn him. I was surrounded by people who loved him. More, I've always been able to talk of him with pride, whereas you...'

'I was proud of him.'

Deep breath. 'If you were proud of him you wouldn't be talking to your nephew about wasting his life surfing.'

'I only suggested—'

'It's not your place to suggest.'

'Kelly, he'll have nothing,' he exploded. 'Heaven knows whether he can get that leg strong enough to go back to competitive surfing but even if he can, there'll be more accidents, there'll be the natural aging of his body, there'll be life. How can he possibly earn enough to buy himself a decent home, a decent future.'

'He's able to sort that himself,' she snapped. 'He's a smart kid and he knows what he's doing. But even so…is a decent future predicated on a house like yours?'

'Yes,' he said, sounding goaded. 'It'd be his, something he can control, a sanctuary that can't be taken away from him.'

'Lying on the surfboard at dawn is something that can't be taken away from him as well. Friends, a community, that's something, too.'

'It's not enough. You need a home.'

'We never have.'

'I don't know how you've existed.'

'We've done more than exist. We've been happy.'

'So you're condemning him to a lifetime of being a nomad?'

'Me?' She met his gaze head on. 'You think I should be dictating my son's life? As your father dictated yours?'

'He didn't.'

'I think he did,' she said evenly. 'He drove Jess away and he made you so fearful that you put your home above everything. It's not your retreat, Matt, it's your prison.'

'How can you say that?'

'This hospital is a goldfish bowl.' If he was going to make assumptions about her son, she could throw a few home truths back. 'Everyone talks about everyone. They say you spend more time with your house and your dogs than with your friends—that you don't get close. They say your marriage didn't last because you held yourself aloof. You have a reputation for being a loner, for helping others but never asking for help yourself. You care for your patients but you care for solitude above all else.'

'Is that what everyone says?'

'Yes,' she said evenly. 'And I reject your life plan. My son is a lovely social kid who cares about the world. He's surrounded by his friends. Even though he's a long way away, he has people Skyping him on the computer at all hours. He's not depressed, like his father. He's not obsessed with possessions, like his uncle. Do you think he'd be desolated if he was living in that dreary little apartment I found first? As long as we'd got rid of the bugs he'd hardly notice.'

'He loves my home.'

'Yes, but if you asked him to choose home or his friends, it'd be his friends in a heartbeat. That's how I've raised him, and I'm proud of the man he's turning into. He's healthy and he's happy and I won't have you judging him.'

'We're worlds apart on this one.'

'Yes, we are,' she said, and somehow she managed to keep her voice even, she managed to keep her twisted heart under some sort of control. She'd held this man in her arms. For a short time she'd thought…she'd thought…

Well, enough of thinking. She needed to act on evidence, not emotion.

'We are worlds apart,' she told him sadly. 'I guess it doesn't matter, though. We've lived in separate worlds all our lives. As soon as Jess is better we'll do so again. But, please, until then keep your judgement under control. I'd love Jess to know he has an uncle; a link with the father he never knew. If you can figure some way to relate to him without your prejudices getting in the way, it'd be great, but don't interfere. I won't risk him ending up like you or his father. As for you and me…what was between us must have been only that. Temptation. Sex. A stupid rush of blood to the head. So now we put it aside. I need to keep Jess safe and if I'm to do that, you and I don't take what's between us any further.'

Did she think he was a danger to Jess? Did she think he could pressure the kid into illness? The thought left him cold.

'What's between you and Mom?' Jess asked him. It was a Sunday. He was out on the veranda, watching Kelly walking down on the beach, when Jess thumped his way out to talk to him.

'What do you mean?'

'I mean every time you're near she puts on this weird smiley face and takes the first excuse to escape. I know things have been non-existent between Dad's family since I was born but now Mom's acting as if you're a threat.'

'I can't see that I'm a threat.'

'You did threaten to send me back to school. I'm over that, but Mom still seems scared.'

Scared… Over and over the word echoed.

Eighteen years ago he'd blamed himself when his brother had died. He hadn't done enough.

He should step back now.

'Maybe it's my family,' he offered. 'Your grandfather's a powerful man. He likes control. If he knew you existed he'd want some sort of control.'

'He doesn't control you.'

'It's taken a lot to get away from him.'

'He wouldn't control us, and I don't think Mom's scared of him. I think she's scared of you.'

'She has no reason to be.'

'That's what I told her,' Jess said. 'But, still, whenever you're near she sort of freezes. I don't understand.'

'Neither do I.'

'Then talk to her about it,' Jess said, irritated. 'It's messing with my serenity.'

'Your serenity?' Matt said, startled, and the boy grinned.

'She's cool, my mom,' he said. 'But she's supposed to worry about me, not the other way round. I'd appreciate it if you could fix it.'

He headed back to his video games, leaving Matt to his thoughts.

Fix it. How was he supposed to do that? A chasm seemed to have opened up between them that he didn't have a clue how to cross. Okay, he understood her fears, but how could she not see how important a home, a base, was? Jess was at risk of ending up with nothing.

Matt's career and his home had given him power over his father. For Jess not to have that same power seemed appalling. Kelly was scared, but there was more than one path to disaster.

This was a deep divide and it meant he couldn't do what Jess wanted. It was messing with Jess's serenity, but it was also doing more. It was causing a man and woman to stand apart.

Maybe it was just as well. He'd had one failed marriage and he still didn't fully understand the cause. Maybe he was meant to be a loner. He had his dogs and his home and his career. What more could a man want?

A woman like Kelly?

No.

He went to work, he came home and he avoided Kelly. She was always on the edge of his consciousness but he'd made a decision.

He'd been a loner for ever and it couldn't stop now.

* * *

If it wasn't for Matt Eveldene she might even be enjoying this forced pause in her life, this time dictated by Jess's accident. Her days were full. Every morning she dropped Jess at the hospital rehab unit. He spent the next few hours working with the physios, exercising to keep his muscles from wasting and making friends in the process. Jess enjoyed his mornings and so did she. Her work in Emergency was varied. She was often run off her feet. She felt useful, the staff were friendly, and it was only Matt's occasional presence that caused her unease.

She didn't know how to handle the way he made her feel. When he walked into the ward it was like she had brain freeze. She had no idea why he made her feel like that, but he did and she didn't like it.

She liked the afternoons, when she took Jess home, when they had the house and the beach to themselves and she knew Matt was at work and wouldn't disturb their peace. Jess mostly snoozed and played computer games. She swam and read and felt...like she was home?

It was a great place, she conceded. It was indeed a lovely home. But for Matt to say it was all-important... For Matt to pressure Jess because he might not be able to afford a home like this... It clearly showed the gulf between them—the gulf that had killed Matt's brother?

Things weren't important. Her attitude to Matt was right. She tried to tell herself that. His house—his *home*—was amazing, but it couldn't be put above all else.

Forget it.

But she couldn't relax. Her body didn't know how to. As soon as Matt returned she retreated to her side of the house. He was her landlord; anything else was too threatening.

Until the day of the suicide.

* * *

Mid-morning. Friday. Outside the day was gorgeous. 'I hate not being able to surf,' Jess had grumbled as she'd driven them both to the hospital, and she'd agreed. Today was a perfect day to be outside. A perfect day to live.

But for the boy who was wheeled into Emergency at six minutes past ten the day must have seemed anything but perfect. The ligature marks on his neck were raw and appalling. The paramedics were still working frantically as they wheeled him in, but Kelly took one look and knew they were too late.

Beth did the initial assessment and Kelly, standing behind her, ready to move into resuscitation mode the moment Beth said the word, was relieved that it was Beth who had to shake her head, Beth who had to remove the cardiac patches, close her eyes briefly and say, 'I'm so sorry, guys, but we've lost this one. Thank you for trying.'

The police arrived.

And Matt.

She briefly remembered that Beth had called Matt down to see to an elderly patient's hip fracture. He stood at the inner door to Emergency and took the scene in at a glance. They were wheeling the kid into a private cubicle but everyone still seemed paralysed with horror.

A middle-aged couple came through the outer entrance. They stopped and stood still, as if terrified to enter. The boy's parents? The man was in work overalls and heavy boots, clothes that said he was a builder or similar. The woman was all in white, dressed for lawn bowls. They were holding each other for support but not giving it to each other. They looked bewildered, shocked to the point of collapse.

Kelly took a deep, fast breath. She glanced through to Beth, knew she was caught up with the police, and knew the job of caring for the parents fell to her. She walked towards them, signalling to a nurse to help.

The nurse stepped forward but then stopped, put her hand to her mouth and shook her head wildly. She retreated fast.

Vomiting was what Kelly felt like doing. The angle of the boy's neck…the horror of that ligature…

He was, what? Twenty maybe? Young enough to be the nurse's brother.

Or husband?

Hold it together, she told herself harshly. You're no use if you can't keep emotion in check. If you can't suppress history flooding back.

The older of the paramedics was still there, grim faced and silent. She took his clipboard and searched for what she needed.

Toby Ryan. Aged nineteen. Found by the surf-club manager in the club storeroom half an hour ago.

'Positive ID?' she asked, and the paramedic nodded.

'The surf-club manager knows him. Seems he's been a club member since he was a nipper.'

There was no question, then. She knew what she had to do. She turned back to face the parents.

'Mr and Mrs Ryan?'

It was the woman who found the strength to nod.

'Y-yes.'

What had they been told?

Assume nothing.

'Toby's your son?'

'Yes.' The woman closed her eyes and put her hand up as if to ward off what was coming.

'Come through where we can be private,' she said gently.

They already knew. Someone must have phoned them;

someone from the surf club? The woman's legs were giving way under her.

Kelly moved to catch her before she sagged, but Matt was there before her, catching her under the arm, holding her upright.

'I have her,' he said. 'You help Mr Ryan. This way, sir.'

Together they led them into the counselling room, set up for just this purpose. It held a settee and two big armchairs and a maxi box of tissues. The woman slumped onto the settee, stared at the tissues and moaned. Her husband sat beside her, clasped his hands and stared at the floor.

'I knew it'd come to this,' he whispered. 'We've been dreading this day. Was it…was it quick?'

'Yes,' Kelly said, thinking of the snapped vertebrae. 'Almost instant.'

'Did a good job, then,' the man said heavily.

'Sir…' Matt said, but the man glared at him as if he was the enemy.

'Call me Doug,' he snapped. 'And Lizzie. We're Toby's Mum and Dad. There's no "sir" about it. No bloody formality today. No bureaucrats. No one helped our Toby. No one could.'

'We knew it was coming.' Lizzie was talking to herself. She was a dumpy little woman in crisp bowling whites, and the life seemed to have been sucked out of her. It was as if a ghost was talking.

'He was born with it, we reckon,' she whispered. 'The black dog. It wouldn't let up. Wherever he went, whatever he did, it kept coming back. Black, black, black. We couldn't help him. His sisters, his brother, all our family. We love him so much. We love him and love him and we can't help. We don't know what to do.'

Her segue into the present tense, where her son was still alive, where problems were still here, still now, seemed to catch her, and for Kelly it was too much. Professional detachment be damned. She was down on her knees, gathering the woman into her arms and hugging her close.

'There's nothing more you can do except keep on loving him,' she whispered, as she held and the woman sobbed and the man beside her groaned his anguish. 'You've done everything you could and Toby knows that. You love him and that's all that counts. The disease has killed him, but that's what it was, a disease. It's tearing your heart out, but what stays is your love for your son. You did everything you could. You couldn't defeat it but no matter what's happened, Toby's love will stay with you for ever.'

Matt had an afternoon of consultation booked but he cancelled. His secretary took one look at his face and didn't ask questions. Kelly finished at one, and he was in the car park, waiting for her. Jess was already in the car.

'Disaster of a morning,' he'd told Jess. 'A kid of your father's age when he died was brought in. Suicide. And your mother had to deal with it. We're taking her home. We'll come back later and pick up the Jeep.'

'Mom's tough,' Jess said. 'Stuff doesn't upset her much.'

Yeah? Matt saw his Kelly's face as she emerged from Emergency and he knew Jess was wrong. A cameraman and a reporter were waiting at the door. Toby had been a surf coach, popular and involved in the community. His death would hit the local news. The camera flashed, the reporter pressed forward but she extricated herself, fast.

She was some woman.

'Kelly?' He headed toward her, ignoring the media. She glanced up and saw him and her face relaxed a little.

'I need to fetch Jess.'

'We're both here,' Matt said gently. 'We're taking you home.'

'There's no need.'

'There's every need.'

'Hey, Mom,' Jess said, as she reached the car.

Her face crumpled then. She'd been keeping up a front, he saw. She'd probably been planning to keep on the same coping face she'd used for her son for years, but Jess's concern had slipped behind her defences.

She reached out and hugged him and Jess let himself be hugged.

Then she had herself together, hauling back, swiping her face and giving a shame-faced smile.

'It's okay. It's just…'

'Matt says a guy died just like Dad.'

'I… Yes.'

'I can't imagine how you must feel,' Jess said, and Matt looked at Jess and thought this kid was seventeen but suddenly he sounded like a man.

He wanted to hug them both. A lot.

He couldn't. He was on the outside, looking in.

'I'm playing chauffeur,' he asserted. 'The crutches get to ride up front with me. You guys travel in the back.'

'I can drive,' Kelly said. 'I don't need—'

'You do need,' he said harshly. 'You've needed for eighteen years and I've done nothing. Get in the car, Kelly, and let me help.'

She did. He drove them home, the back way, not past the surf club, where police cars would still be clustered, but through the hills behind town. Jess set up a stream of small talk in the back seat, though actually it wasn't small talk, it was all about his rehabilitation, about what Patsy, the rehab physician, had told him, about how the strengthening exercises were going and what he could reasonably hope for as he healed. Getting such information from a teenager was normally like pulling teeth, so Kelly was forced to listen, forced to respond, and Matt saw a tinge of colour return to her face.

He gave Jess a thumbs-up via the rear-view mirror, and

Jess gave him a return man-to-man nod and went right on distracting his mother.

He was a kid to be proud of, Matt thought. A son to be proud of?

And right there, right then, he realised how much he loved the pair of them. What was he on about, pushing the kid to do what he thought was important? He watched the pair of them and he thought they knew what was important. If they wanted to surf every day of their lives, who was he to judge? Whatever they did, it was okay by him.

And more. Whatever they did, he wanted to join them.

But now wasn't the time for declarations. Now was simply the time for being in the background, giving them space, but he glanced back and saw the way Jess held his mother's hand, saw the way she tried to smile at him, saw the deep concern in the kid's eyes for his mom and he thought...

He thought for the first time in his life, he desperately wanted to share.

CHAPTER TEN

SHE SPENT THE afternoon trying to work things out in her own mind. Matt was nowhere to be seen. She made Jess hamburgers for tea, and then, as he settled in with Matt's dogs and his computer games, she gave him a hug and made her decision.

'I need to go talk to Matt.'

'Of course you do,' Jess said, not taking his eyes from his game. 'He's shattered, too.'

'You think?'

'Yeah,' Jess said. 'When he came to get me in physio he looked like he'd been wiped out and held under for ten minutes. Well, maybe not ten,' he corrected himself, 'but three. Time enough to see his life rolling before his eyes.'

'What do you know about life rolling before your eyes?' Kelly demanded, startled, and Jess grinned.

'Hey, I've lived through a Very Bad Accident. When I felt that board crack against me I thought of all the levels of *Major Mayhem* I had yet to play. It was a sobering experience.'

She gave him a pretend slap to the side of the head and chuckled.

'So you don't mind if I go and see Matt now?'

'Stay the night,' Jess offered. 'I'm a big boy now.'

'Jess!'

'Seriously, Mom,' Jess said, and finally he turned away from his computer game. 'Matt's great and he cares. Don't let me—or Dad—get in the way of something beautiful.'

'Beautiful?' she choked.

He grinned. 'Heart and flowers and violins. Yuck.' But then he sobered. 'Or just real good friends. Go for it, Mom. Think of yourself for once.'

Right.

It was a discombobulating little speech, and she was still feeling discombobulated when she headed out onto the veranda.

Matt was sitting on the settee, holding a beer, staring out at the moonlight.

'Pa Kettle,' she said cautiously. 'You need to make that settee a rocker.'

'I need my dogs,' he said. 'Traitors.'

'Jess has popcorn. No contest.'

He grinned and went to rise.

'Don't get up.' She perched beside him. 'I need to talk.'

'So do I.'

'Me first,' she said, and then she paused because all of a sudden it seemed hard. Matt watched her in the moonlight, then left her and came back with a glass of wine. She took it and swirled it in his gorgeous crystal glass and thought of all the chipped and cracked kitchenware she and Jess had used over the years. And then she thought, it didn't matter. It didn't matter one bit.

People were what was important. This man was important.

Up until now her hurt had all been about herself and her son. Somehow today had made her see that long-ago devastating scene in the funeral parlour in a different light. It made sense of the tie Matt had with things rather than people and it had exposed the knot of hurt and pain this man had carried for years.

Today she'd looked at the shattered parents and she'd known that she couldn't protect Jess, any more than Matt could have protected his brother.

'You know it wasn't your fault,' she said into the stillness, and the words seemed to freeze and hang. 'What happened to Jess... Today I looked at Toby and I saw a kid who had everything. Loving parents. Sisters and brother who adored him. After you left Toby's sister came in and she talked and talked, and I had time to let her. Toby was loved. Whatever he did was fine by them. He had his beloved surf club. He had his whole community behind him, but the depression, the illness wouldn't let go. His family knew this was coming, she said. It was like watching a slow train coming toward them and not being able to get off the track. Doctors, treatments, everything that could be done was done. And yet the depression won.'

'Kelly—'

'No, let me say it,' she said. 'I've been angry. I lost my Jess and then you came and you were the embodiment of all the things I thought had caused Jess to die. Jess used to talk about your house, the Eveldene mansion. He used to talk about all the things he had, all the things your family valued, as if they were the cause. So when you came, I hated you and I hated what you represented. I swore my Jess would never learn your values. Then...what happened between us...somehow it felt like a betrayal, and what you said to Jess made it worse.

'But today, maybe for the first time, I figured out how unfair my anger was. Your suggestion that Jess study was just a suggestion. It was nothing to make a big deal over. And as for eighteen years ago... You were a kid yourself. You were doing what your father should have done, but even that's immaterial. What matters is that today I let go of my anger. Eighteen years and it's finally gone.'

'One kid's death…' he said slowly, but she shook her head.

'No. It's lots of things. How the hospital staff react to you. Your kindness toward your patients. The fact that you care. The way you've treated Jess, and then stepped back when you realised you'd hurt him. And this afternoon I finally figured it out. You've been hurting as much as I have. It's a no-brainer yet finally I've seen it. You loved Jess. You lost him and now you hold on to things instead. Like this house. This place. Your career. Tangible things are important but it's not because you're impersonal. It's anything but. It's because once upon a time you saw your brother on a slab in a mortuary and part of you died.'

And something within him twisted, so hard it was as if things were ripping apart. The pain of the last eighteen years. The way he'd reacted to this woman the first time he'd seen her, with such unforgivable anger. The aching helplessness of knowing his big brother had been self-destructing and there hadn't been a thing he could do about it.

Something changed.

He stood abruptly, knocking the beer at his feet so it spilled its contents. Who cared? He didn't. Where to go from here? So many emotions, coalescing in one morning's tragedy. In one woman's words.

'Kelly, maybe that was what I was going to tell you,' he managed. He was trying to figure it for himself. How to put it into words.

'I did blame myself,' he said. 'I was four years younger than Jess and I ached for him, but every time I tried to do anything I had to retreat. My dad reacted with anger, but Jess himself retreated. I ached because he asked me to come to Hawaii when I finished school. He sent me the plane fare. But I was eighteen. I thought he was on drugs. My father was apoplectic when I even suggested it. It was too hard and I've hated myself for ever because I didn't have the courage to stand up to my father. But today I saw that it wouldn't have made one bit of difference. Nothing I said or did...'

'Nor me,' Kelly said, and she stood beside him and slipped her hand in his. 'We both loved him and somehow we ended up hating each other because of his death. It was dumb. We both ended up rejecting...something that's important.'

He turned to her then, taking her hands so they were locked together in the moonlight.

'You mean...important as making a go of...us?'

'We could give it a try,' she said softly. She ventured a faint smile. 'I might learn to love this house as well.'

'It's a great house.'

Her smile faded. 'Matt...'

'I didn't mean,' he said, 'that this house is as important as people. I didn't mean this house is as important as you.'

'Or happiness?'

'Or happiness.'

'We need to take things slowly.' She bit her lip, looking up at him in the moonlight as if she was trying to read his mind. 'And, Matt...despite what I just said I won't have you lecturing Jess. You need to respect that he's his own person.'

'I will respect that.'

'The truth's in the doing,' she said with a touch of asperity. 'But you're stuck with us for another few weeks. If you let us hang around, I'll see what you're made of.'

'And I'll see what I'm made of, too.'

'No judging?'

'Just loving.'

'It seems,' she said uncertainly, 'that loving's the given. It's fitting everything else in that's the problem.'

'You mean you might love me?'

'I think I might,' she said with all seriousness, and then she gasped as he tugged her close. 'Matt, we have all sorts of stuff we need to work out first.'

'We will work it out. Give us time.' But he spoke thickly because his face was in her hair. He was kissing her, tugging her tightly into him. 'We'll sort it.'

'Matt…' She still sounded worried.

'Let the past go,' he told her, sure of himself now, holding his woman in his arms and knowing nothing else was important. 'There's just us.'

'And Jess and our careers and your dogs and your house…'

'Kelly?'

'Mmm?'

'Is Jess likely to disapprove if I pick you up, cart you to my lair and have my wicked way with you?'

'Jess practically ordered me to submit,' she said. 'And he's just reached the next level in his game. Who's noticing?'

'I'm noticing,' he said, as he swung her into his arms and kissed her, a long, deep kiss that held all the promise of life to come. 'I'm noticing a lot,' he said, as he pushed the door open with his foot. 'I'm noticing and noticing and noticing. But, Dr Kelly Eveldene, all I'm noticing is you.'

'So are we happy-ever-aftering?'

It was the morning after the night before. Kelly was making pancakes on her side of the beige door. She was demurely dressed in her respectable bathrobe. She'd showered, she'd brushed her hair and she was trying hard to look like nothing had changed. She was a mom looking after her kid.

She was different.

'What?' She plated two pancakes for her son. 'What do you mean?'

'I mean you look like the cat that got the canary. Smug R Us. Does Matt look the same?'

'I… He might.' She tried to fight it but she could feel herself blushing from the toes up.

'Excellent,' Jess said. 'He's cool.'

'Didn't he tell you to go back to school?'

'Yeah, but it was only past history that made me react,' he said. 'The way you told me Grandpa treated Dad. I've thought about it. Judging someone because of what happened years ago might be dumb. If we tell him about my—'

'Jess, don't tell him yet,' she said, suddenly urgent.

'Why not?'

'Because if we're to have some sort of future together I want him wanting us, warts and all.'

'Then push him further. You could give up medicine and come surfing. The way he's looking, he might even come, too. I shouldn't say this about my own mother, but you're still hot. He's tempted. Anyone can see it, and you're tempted right back. There's waves of temptation all over the place. Why resist, people? Go for it.'

'Oh, Jess.' Where had this funny, wise, grown-up kid come from?

'So what are you going to do about it?' Jess demanded.

'Maybe I could invite him in for pancakes,' she conceded.

'Why not?' Jess said amiably. 'But don't stop there. Why not knock a hole in the wall and be done with it?'

He had everything he wanted, here, now. Kelly was living in his house. She was part of his life. It was like he'd been missing a part of himself and the part had fitted back together, making him complete.

'Jess says I look like the cat that got the canary,' she told him, lying in his arms on Sunday morning. 'I think you do, too.'

'You're an extraordinarily beautiful canary.'

'I'm a happy canary,' she said, and snuggled down against him. 'Did you know you have the most beautiful body I've ever seen? They should freeze you and use you in anatomy lessons. Perfect male specimen. Plastic surgeons, eat your hearts out.'

'They can have me in fifty years.'

'Okay,' she said. 'I expect you'll still be perfect in fifty years. Goodness, though, think of all the things we'll have done in the interim. You might have a few life scars.'

'We both might,' he said, tugging her closer still. 'But they can't make you less than beautiful. They'll be shared scars.'

'I want to visit the Amazon,' she said, running her fingers down his chest in a way that made his whole body feel alive. 'You want to risk a few mosquito bites?'

'The Amazon?'

'One day. It's just…single mom, medicine, there's never been time or money for anything else. You want a few adventures with me?'

'I'm pretty happy where I am, right now,' he said, and she drew away slightly.

'That sounds like the man who loves his house.'

'I'll take you to the Amazon.'

'You'll want to come to the Amazon? It's different.'

'I guess it is.'

'Matt…'

'Mmm?'

'Will we be all right?'

'We'll be all right,' he said, and kissed her and knew he'd do whatever it took to keep this woman in his arms.

For ever.

They loved, they slept, things were perfect, but there was this niggle. This faint unease.

She was slotting into his perfect life. Jess had suggested she throw in medicine and go surfing to test him, but he didn't need testing.

He was her gorgeous Matt, and she'd love him for ever. She'd do whatever it took.

Would he?

It was a tiny niggle. She should put it aside. It was nothing, not when he held her, not when he loved her, not when his loving swept all aside in its wonder.

And then his parents came.

It was late Sunday morning. They'd surfed, dressed, breakfasted, and were sitting on the veranda, feeling smug.

'We need two rockers,' Kelly said, pushing away that stupid, worrying niggle. 'It's not just Pa Kettle. It's Ma and Pa and the whole domestic set-up.'

'Sounds pretty perfect,' Matt said, but then the helicopter hovered into view, and to their mutual astonishment it came down to land on their beach.

'What the...?' Matt said, and rose and stared down the cliff track. And then he swore. 'Dad!'

Dad. Henry Eveldene.

Kelly was wearing shorts, T-shirt and bare feet. Her hair was still damp from their swim.

She wanted to be in hospital whites, she thought. She wanted to be professional, in charge of her world, in a position to face this man on her own terms.

But this was her own terms, she told herself. It had to be.

Jess had limped out of the house with the dogs to see what was happening. She reached behind her and grabbed his hand.

This wasn't threatening, she told herself. This was an elderly couple. How scary could they be?

The woman didn't look scary. She was tiny, seemingly frail, dressed in a plain blue skirt and white shirt, with pearls around her neck, and her white hair caught up into a soft bun with curls escaping. This must be Rose, Jess's mother.

Henry was almost her polar opposite, stout and business-suited. Bald, red faced and already looking angry, he was striding up the path to the house as if he was wielding a battering ram. Rose was struggling behind.

Matt strode down to meet them, heading straight past his father to gather his mother into a hug. 'Mum!'

'Matt,' Rose whispered, and put a hand to his hair as if assuring herself he was real. But she was ignored by her husband. Henry was obviously here on a mission.

'Who the hell is she?' Henry demanded, booming loudly enough to be heard on the next beach. He shaded his eyes and stared up at the house at Kelly. 'Is that her?'

'Is that who?'

'Kelly Eveldene.' He hauled a newspaper clipping from his breast pocket and waved it angrily at Matt. 'You know I have shares in half the country's local papers and I have a notify order if the name Eveldene ever comes up. Dr Kelly Eveldene was named as treating doctor for a kid who sui-cided. Based in the hospital you're working at. I called the hospital. It took three calls and a bribe and then I found out she was living with you. With you!' He stared up at the veranda again, at Kelly.

And then he saw the boy beside her.

'Jess.'

The word came out as a strangled gasp but it wasn't from Henry. It was from Rose.

Kelly had seen this woman's picture. It had been in Jess's wallet when he'd died. Sometimes she still looked at it, and Rose's face still smiled out.

Rose wasn't smiling now. Her face was bleached white. 'Jess,' she said again, and possibly she would have crum-pled if Matt wasn't holding her.

'Mum,' Matt said, and the way he said it was like a caress. 'I was wondering when this should happen, and I'm so glad it finally has. Mum, this is Jessie's son. He's called Jessie, too, and he's your grandson. And this is Kelly. Kelly was Jessie's wife. They're family.'

And he said 'family' so strongly, so surely, that Kelly's world settled. It was an all-encompassing statement, a word that included her for ever.

But it seemed that Henry Eveldene didn't think so. His breath drew in in a hiss of shock and fury. 'What nonsense is this?'

'It's not nonsense,' Matt said evenly. 'Jess married Kelly eighteen years ago. You knew that, Dad.'

'My Jess…married?' Rose gasped, and Matt's grip on her tightened.

'Dad made a decision not to tell you,' Matt said. 'He thought you were shocked enough. It was the wrong decision. We made a lot of wrong decisions back then.'

'Jess's son…' She sounded dazed beyond belief.

'Hey, Grandma.' Jess was a typical teenager, ignoring undercurrents, listening to everything with his typical insouciance. 'I've always wanted a grandma. Cool. And… Grandpa?'

'I am not your grandfather.' It was a roar of rage that made even Jess blink. 'If you're after money…'

'What are you on about?' Jess asked, astounded, and Rose gave a moan of pain.

'No one's after money,' Matt snapped.

'I paid you off,' Henry roared, directing his fury straight at Kelly. 'You cashed that cheque and the deal was that you kept out of our lives for ever.'

'But Jess's insurance policy belonged to his wife.' Still Matt spoke evenly, and Kelly recognised that he'd faced down his father's fury before. Matt went on, his voice stern. 'That money belonged to Kelly, no matter what we decided. We had no right to claim otherwise. We had no right to put conditions on it.'

But Henry wasn't listening. He couldn't hear past his fury. 'So now you've come crawling back, wanting more—'

'That's enough, Dad,' Matt snapped. 'Kelly and Jess want nothing.'

'You're giving them a place to stay.'

'Yes, but—'

'And what does the boy do? Nothing, like his father?'

'He surfs,' Matt said through gritted teeth.

And Kelly thought she should say something and then she thought, No. She could walk away. This fury was between Matt and his father.

'Surfs…' The word came out like the worst of oaths.

'Dad, leave this. You're shocked,' Matt said. 'Don't say anything you might regret. Come up and meet them.'

'You have no right to be here,' the man snapped at Kelly.

'She has every right.'

'And you're calling yourself a doctor,' Henry spat at Kelly. 'You're not even qualified to practise in Australia. I did a fast check before I came. *Dr* Eveldene. Qualified in Hawaii. Do you intend practising in Australia? Ha! I have influence. If you think I can't get you kicked out of this country, you're dead wrong.'

'Dad, what's Kelly ever done to hurt you?' Matt demanded.

'What she's done is immaterial. I have no idea what her game is but I want no part of it. Jess married her when he was a drug-addicted nut case. The marriage should never have been allowed and we owe her nothing. Whatever story she's conned you with, it's to end. She can get out of this country, now.'

But there was another player in this drama. Rose. The elderly woman's eyes hadn't left Jess.

'Henry, stop yelling,' she said, in a strange, wandering voice that somehow cut across her husband's anger. 'Matt, you're saying Jess had a son?'

'This is nothing to do with us,' Henry snapped.

'But it has!' Rose was stumbling over her words. 'Of course it has. My son had a son? Oh, Matt, why didn't you tell us?'

'I didn't know,' Matt said.

'But you knew about Kelly?'

'I… Yes.'

'But you didn't tell us about her either.'

'Dad knew. He thought the truth would break your heart.'

'But my heart had already broken,' Rose whispered. 'When Jess died.'

And Kelly's heart twisted, just like that. Anger was forgotten. No matter what had gone before, this was a woman who'd lost her son.

'Your Jess carried your photograph in his wallet for all the time I knew him,' she said, speaking directly to Rose and ignoring the crimson-faced bully beside her. 'He had it with him when he died. He spoke of you often, with love. I honoured your husband's wishes not to contact you but now it's happened, I'm glad.' She gripped Jess's hand. 'This is your grandson. No matter what's gone on before, surely that's all that matters.'

'It is,' Matt said strongly. 'Dad, our family has treated Kelly appallingly. It's time for it to stop.'

But Henry Eveldene wasn't done. He'd obviously had twenty-four hours knowing who Kelly must be. Twenty-four hours to work himself into a rage. It'd be part guilt induced, Kelly thought, trying hard to be compassionate. He'd rejected his son. To now embrace his son's wife and his grandson would be acknowledging something that was possibly unbearable.

'There's not one reason for it to stop,' he snapped.

'There's a hundred reasons,' Matt snapped back. 'And not one reason why it has to continue. What is it, Dad? Why can't you accept Jess's family?'

'Jess has no family.' The words were a blast that rang over the cliffs and out to the sea beyond. Down on the beach the helicopter pilot stood by his machine, waiting.

Kelly thought idly, I wonder what he thinks of this family reunion?

Not much, probably. After all, it wasn't much of a family.

'You've broken your pledge. I'll drum you out of the country,' Henry snarled.

But still Kelly was calm. How much self-hatred must lie behind his bluster? She was feeling weird, almost analytical. This man had no power to hurt her.

But Rose... She looked at the elderly woman's distressed face and she thought she couldn't distress her further.

'You won't need to drum me out of the country,' she said. 'We're only here because my Jess broke his leg, surfing.'

'Surfing...' Henry spat, as if the word was foul.

'Surfing,' Kelly continued, cutting over his rage. 'We're stuck here for another few weeks. Matt has been kind and we'll always be grateful, but we acknowledge how you feel. I don't want Jess to have any part of your anger. We'll leave as soon as he's healed, and we won't come back.'

'Kelly...' Matt released his mother, and in a few long strides he was on the veranda. 'No!'

'I want no part of this.'

'Yeah, we don't have to cop this,' Jessie said.

'Leave it, Matt,' Kelly said. 'We want no part of a family feud.'

'It's bullshit,' Jess said.

And Matt stood beside these two who had come to mean so much to him, he looked down at his parents, and he thought that's exactly what this was. Bullshit. He might not have used the teenager's expression but right now it seemed to fit.

But there was no way he could stop this viciousness. His father was powerful. He had contacts in every media outlet in the land. If there was anything in Kelly's past to be dragged up, he'd find it.

Kelly had spent her childhood in a strange, unconventional environment. There'd be things his father could use and he would use them. He'd twist them, he'd spit them out in any form that suited him. He could do real damage.

And he looked again at Kelly, at the tilt of her chin, at her defiance, and he thought of all the other ogres she'd had to face beside his father. He'd been one of them.

No more, he thought, right there and then. This woman was no longer alone. His father was attacking her and it was personal. She was family.

She was his family.

His love.

'If Kelly goes, I go,' he said, into the sun-washed day, and the world seemed to pause at his words. 'I'll leave the country to be with her.'

Kelly gasped. She opened her mouth to speak and nothing came out.

Nothing, nothing and nothing.

Inevitably, it Jess who was first to recover. He had teenage resilience. Teenage enthusiasm.

'You want to come back to Hawaii with us? Cool.' Ignoring the tension around them, he launched himself straight into the future. 'I can show you the best surf spots. The Pipeline's awesome but there are even better places. Matt, it'll be great.'

But Kelly was staring at him as if he'd slapped her.

'You can't…you can't be serious?'

But he looked into her eyes and he'd never been so serious in his life. Everything else faded but his need to say it like it was.

By his side, Bess and Spike were standing very still, as if they, too, knew this moment was life-changing. What were the requirements for taking dogs abroad? He'd need to find out. No matter, that was detail. What mattered now was taking that look of disbelief from Kelly's face.

He fought for the right words and he found them, maybe not word perfect but close enough. He said them now, with all the love that shone through the centuries since the vow had first been made.

'"Whither thou goest, I will go,"' he said softly. '"Thy home will be my home and thy people shall be my people."'

'Matt…' She could hardly breathe. 'Matt, you can't.'

'Why can't I?'

'This is your home.' She gestured around, to the house he'd built with such love and such pride. This house that had been so important to him but now seemed nothing compared to what he felt for this woman.

'I think…' he said softly. 'I hope that my home is you.'

'But you love this house,' she breathed.

'I love you more.'

'You can't.'

'I can't think of a single reason why I can't. I can think of a hundred reasons why I can.'

'You and your hundred reasons,' she said, her eyes misting with tears, her voice cracked with emotion. 'I bet you can't.'

'Shall I start? Number one, you make excellent pancakes. And hamburgers. We'll forget about cakes. Two, anyone who sees you in a bathing suit will be in love in an instant. Three, your chuckle does something to my insides that leaves me breathless. Four...'

'This could get boring,' Jess said, grinning.

'Not...it's not boring,' Kelly managed. 'I like it.'

'Are you out of your mind?' The baffled roar from beneath the veranda made them all pause. Henry looked as if he was about to explode. 'What nonsense is this? This woman's leaving.'

'With me,' Matt said evenly, and then, because it seemed the right thing to do, the only thing to do, because Kelly's eyes were still confused, because their whole future seemed to hang on this moment, he did what any sane man would do.

He caught her hands and tugged her round to face him. And he dropped to one knee.

'Kelly Eveldene,' he said, strongly and surely, 'will you marry me?'

'Wow,' Jess whooped. 'Wow and wow and wow. Mom, say yes.'

'If she says yes I won't have a son,' Henry roared.

'If she says yes I'll have my own son,' Matt said evenly, his eyes not leaving Kelly's face. 'If Jess will have me.'

'Only if you increase my allowance,' Jess said, and grinned.

'Done,' Matt said grandly, and then looked a bit uneasy. 'Hang on. By how much?'

'We'll negotiate,' Jess said. 'What do they call it? A marriage settlement.'

'Have your lawyers speak to my lawyers,' Matt said, and he was smiling, but he didn't take his eyes from Kelly. 'Love?'

'You can't,' she whispered, and she knelt to join him. 'To leave everything...your career, your gorgeous house, your place in life...'

'People are what's important,' he said, knowing that

finally he had it. Kelly held everything important to him, in her smile, in her courage, in her life.

A hundred reasons? There must be a thousand, he thought, and more to come. He had a lifetime of learning how to love this woman. A lifetime of being loved in return.

'Kelly, if you can…'

'You mean it?'

'More than anything else in the world.'

'Then of course I can,' she said, caught between laughter and tears. 'Oh, Matt, I love you. I love you and love you and love you. Do I need to make that a hundred times, too?'

'Three will do,' he said grandly. 'We have all the time in the world to make it up to a hundred. Or a thousand or a million or whatever comes next.'

'We're not making sense.'

'I guess we're not. But you will be my wife?'

'Yes.'

'Then that's all the sense I need. Everything else will follow.'

And finally she was being kissed, deeply, soundly, possessively, and she was kissing back with every single emotion returned in full.

How did she love this man?

For a while she'd thought it was to do with her old love, but it wasn't that. When she'd first married she'd been a child. Her husband had been her saviour and her hero. What she felt for this man was far, far different. It was an adult's love and acceptance.

This man was flawed. He'd been hurt, he'd retired to solitude, he'd built walls around himself. She thought of his failed marriage and knew that he'd probably hurt people himself.

He wouldn't now. She knew that with the same surety she knew her love for him wouldn't fail. He'd shed his armour, he'd opened himself to her, and he was hers. He was her gorgeous wounded warrior, as scarred by life as she was, but ready now to step forward. With her.

He loved her and she loved him. All the love in the world was in this kiss. The years ahead stretched gloriously and she thought, I can love, I can love, I can love.

She did love. She was being kissed until her toes curled and nothing else mattered. Nothing, nothing, nothing.

Except…there was the odd spectator or two. Two dogs, Jess, her…parents-in-law? The helicopter pilot down on the beach?

The world.

Somehow they broke apart but not far. Matt's arms still held her. They rose and she looked down at the couple below and felt sad for the pair of them.

'I'm sorry,' she whispered. 'I didn't mean this to happen.'

'Hey, but it's great.' Jess was practically bouncing. 'But I'm not being a pageboy. Think again, people.'

'But I can see you as a ring bearer in pantaloons,' Kelly said. Matt choked and Jess grabbed a cushion from the settee and tossed it at her. But there were still things to be said. Matt fielded the cushion before it reached his beloved and tossed it back. Then he turned to his parents.

'That's it,' he said, in a voice he hadn't known he possessed until now. He'd never known he could feel so sure. 'It's settled so take it or leave it. I'm sorry, Mum,' he said, gentling as he addressed his mother. 'I know this is a huge amount to toss at you in one hit, but Dad's lied to you for years.

'To my shame, I haven't told you about Kelly either. But no more lies. I loved my big brother and I lost him, as you did, but Kelly lost her husband, and her loss matched yours. She was left with a baby to care for on her own. That she's brought him here now, into my life, is a gift beyond price, and that I've fallen in love with her makes things perfect. Kelly and I are family now, and so is Jess. Mum, I still love you, but my way is with Kelly.'

Once more there was silence. But it was okay, Kelly thought, dazed beyond belief.

She wasn't sure what had just happened. She needed space. She needed to go and lock herself in her room and think it all out.

She'd quite like to take Matt to her room with her.

No. Now was not the appropriate time to jump her man. But he *was* her man. Her fiancé. Her soon-to-be husband. Soon she could jump him whenever she wanted—for the rest of her life?

The thought was so overpowering that she felt herself gasp. Matt glanced sharply at her and then he grinned. Could he read her mind? She hoped not, but she met his glinting laughter and she knew…

Happy ever after was right here by her side.

'We're leaving.' Henry's words cut across the intimacy between them. He had no way of hurting them, Kelly thought, but then she glanced at Matt and saw him look at his mother and flinch.

Rose was losing another son.

But maybe not. Henry had grasped Rose's arm, hauling her round to march her down the cliff path, but Rose was balking. Her sensible shoes dug into the track, and when he gave her another, harder tug she wrenched away. She dug her toes in further, as if creating a wedge that would keep her here.

'I have my own money.'

'What are you talking about?' Henry demanded, making to grab her again, but she thrust him off.

'I can do this,' she said. Her faltering words were growing stronger. 'I will. Matt, if you don't mind… If I was to get a little apartment in Hawaii…would you mind if I visited?' She glanced at Jess and her longing was naked for all to see. 'Would it be possible for me to get to know my grandson?'

'What a wonderful idea,' Kelly said, before Matt could answer. Matt was so astounded that he hadn't found his voice. His mother had been a doormat for years, a down-trodden mouse. Suddenly the mouse was squeaking. More, she was laying down ultimatums.

'Don't be ridiculous,' Henry gasped. 'You wouldn't dare.'

'I would dare,' the mouse said, and turned and faced him head on. 'I would dare because Matt and Kelly and Jessie...' Her voice trembled as she said Jessie's name but she made herself continue. 'Matt and Kelly and Jess will be a family, and I want to be part of it.'

CHAPTER ELEVEN

Two months later they left for Hawaii. Not, in the end, to stay, but to visit. Kelly and Jess needed to pack up their apartment and say their goodbyes, and they had another task to do, too.

They carried an urn with them. Matt stood with Jess and his mother and they watched together as Kelly scattered his brother's ashes into the sea at Diamond Head.

This was where Jess had wanted his ashes scattered. Eighteen years later, his ashes had come home.

But this was no longer home for them. They were here to say farewell to a brother, husband, son and father. They were here to let Rose take her fledgling steps as a grandma. Then they were going back to Australia. They were facing Henry's threats down.

'Four against one,' Jess had said. 'We're a family. What threats can possibly mess with us?'

There might be trouble, Matt conceded, but if it came they'd face it together. And Kelly loved his house. His home.

'Let's try,' she'd said. 'The Gold Coast is a perfect place to live. I'm sure I can get full Australian accreditation. Matt, you love it.'

'Not as much as I love you,' he'd growled, but she'd kissed him and held him and smiled.

'Then let's see if we can put it all together as a package,' she'd said. 'Our careers, your house, your dogs, our family. Us. And the university in Brisbane seems great. Jess is already excited about the courses there. It's worth a try.'

And that had been the next shaking of his foundations. His last judgement call shattered. A week after Henry had thrown them his ultimatum, Jess had woken the house with his whooping. It seemed he'd been studying for years, in Hawaii and online when he and his mother were travelling. His exam results—the International Baccalaureate—were through, and meant almost any university course in the world would now be open to him.

'But not until I've surfed for another eighteen months,' Jess told him. 'That's the deal Mum and I made. If I get decent uni entrance exams, Dad's money will fund me for two years on the international surfing tour. She thinks that's what Dad would have wanted.' He'd looked ruefully at his leg. 'I might not make it back to the top,' he conceded, 'but I'll have fun trying. And then, maybe medicine? Maybe architecture. I'm not sure yet, but I have time to plan.'

It had taken Matt's breath away. The pair of them took his breath away. Jess and Kelly. Two astonishing people.

He never ceased to be astonished. And the most astonishing thing was that Kelly loved him. Kelly wanted to be his wife.

And so it was.

Living the dream was what she was doing right now, Kelly thought as she stood by her brand-new husband's side and heard the words that sealed their union for ever.

'I now pronounce you man and wife.'

They were standing on the beach below Matt's house, but this wedding wasn't all about Matt's place in the world. Her world was here, too. They'd timed the wedding so the surfing circuit was back in town, and to her joy a bunch of surfing and doctor friends had made the trip from Hawaii.

Everyone they loved was here, Kelly thought with deep satisfaction. Everyone important.

Even Matt's ex-wife, Jenny, was here with her husband and four kids. She'd flown to the Gold Coast as soon as she'd heard Matt was engaged, and five minutes after meeting Kelly she was beaming.

'I never thought it would happen,' she told Kelly. 'I found it with my Peter but I've always felt sad for Matt. But now... He's smitten. Anyone can see the transformation. Kelly, you're a wonder woman.'

She wasn't a wonder woman, Kelly thought as she and Matt turned to face their friends, hand in hand, man and wife. She was just Kelly. Doctor. Surfer. Mother of Jess. Wife to Matt.

And one extraordinarily happy woman.

'If my chest swells any further I'll bust my tux,' Matt said, and she smiled and smiled.

'Just as well you have your swimming trunks on underneath.'

'I don't. Do you?' he asked, startled.

'Yep. A white bikini.' She spun and showed him the back of her wedding gown. The gown dipped to below her waist, exposing her beautiful bare back, plus the fine cord of a white bikini top, enticingly tied with a bow.

Their audience was cheering, but for this moment they had eyes for only each other. Man and wife, from this day forward.

'Do you think...?' Matt said longingly, touching the bow.

'I do not think,' she said serenely. 'We have two hours' surfing in front of us and photographs, then dinner, the odd speech, then a bit of dancing. There's a hundred reasons why you can't carry me off to your lair right now.'

'There's a thousand reasons why I should.'

'You have time to tell me,' she said, and she couldn't resist. Her new husband had already kissed her, but she was kissing him again. 'You have a lifetime to tell me.'

'It's not long enough,' Matt growled, kissing her back with a passion that brought gasps and laughter from their friends and family. 'All those reasons…I need to start now.'

* * * * *

Mills & Boon® Hardback
March 2014

ROMANCE

A Prize Beyond Jewels	Carole Mortimer
A Queen for the Taking?	Kate Hewitt
Pretender to the Throne	Maisey Yates
An Exception to His Rule	Lindsay Armstrong
The Sheikh's Last Seduction	Jennie Lucas
Enthralled by Moretti	Cathy Williams
The Woman Sent to Tame Him	Victoria Parker
What a Sicilian Husband Wants	Michelle Smart
Waking Up Pregnant	Mira Lyn Kelly
Holiday with a Stranger	Christy McKellen
The Returning Hero	Soraya Lane
Road Trip With the Eligible Bachelor	Michelle Douglas
Safe in the Tycoon's Arms	Jennifer Faye
Awakened By His Touch	Nikki Logan
The Plus-One Agreement	Charlotte Phillips
For His Eyes Only	Liz Fielding
Uncovering Her Secrets	Amalie Berlin
Unlocking the Doctor's Heart	Susanne Hampton

MEDICAL

Waves of Temptation	Marion Lennox
Risk of a Lifetime	Caroline Anderson
To Play with Fire	Tina Beckett
The Dangers of Dating Dr Carvalho	Tina Beckett

0214GEN STD HB

ROMANCE

Million Dollar Christmas Proposal	Lucy Monroe
A Dangerous Solace	Lucy Ellis
The Consequences of That Night	Jennie Lucas
Secrets of a Powerful Man	Chantelle Shaw
Never Gamble with a Caffarelli	Melanie Milburne
Visconti's Forgotten Heir	Elizabeth Power
A Touch of Temptation	Tara Pammi
A Little Bit of Holiday Magic	Melissa McClone
A Cadence Creek Christmas	Donna Alward
His Until Midnight	Nikki Logan
The One She Was Warned About	Shoma Narayanan

HISTORICAL

Rumours that Ruined a Lady	Marguerite Kaye
The Major's Guarded Heart	Isabelle Goddard
Highland Heiress	Margaret Moore
Paying the Viking's Price	Michelle Styles
The Highlander's Dangerous Temptation	Terri Brisbin

MEDICAL

The Wife He Never Forgot	Anne Fraser
The Lone Wolf's Craving	Tina Beckett
Sheltered by Her Top-Notch Boss	Joanna Neil
Re-awakening His Shy Nurse	Annie Claydon
A Child to Heal Their Hearts	Dianne Drake
Safe in His Hands	Amy Ruttan

Mills & Boon® Hardback
April 2014

ROMANCE

A D'Angelo Like No Other	Carole Mortimer
Seduced by the Sultan	Sharon Kendrick
When Christakos Meets His Match	Abby Green
The Purest of Diamonds?	Susan Stephens
Secrets of a Bollywood Marriage	Susanna Carr
What the Greek's Money Can't Buy	Maya Blake
The Last Prince of Dahaar	Tara Pammi
The Sicilian's Unexpected Duty	Michelle Smart
One Night with Her Ex	Lucy King
The Secret Ingredient	Nina Harrington
Her Soldier Protector	Soraya Lane
Stolen Kiss From a Prince	Teresa Carpenter
Behind the Film Star's Smile	Kate Hardy
The Return of Mrs Jones	Jessica Gilmore
Her Client from Hell	Louisa George
Flirting with the Forbidden	Joss Wood
The Last Temptation of Dr Dalton	Robin Gianna
Resisting Her Rebel Hero	Lucy Ryder

MEDICAL

200 Harley Street: Surgeon in a Tux	Carol Marinelli
200 Harley Street: Girl from the Red Carpet	Scarlet Wilson
Flirting with the Socialite Doc	Melanie Milburne
His Diamond Like No Other	Lucy Clark

0314GEN STD HB

Mills & Boon® Large Print
April 2014

ROMANCE

Defiant in the Desert	Sharon Kendrick
Not Just the Boss's Plaything	Caitlin Crews
Rumours on the Red Carpet	Carole Mortimer
The Change in Di Navarra's Plan	Lynn Raye Harris
The Prince She Never Knew	Kate Hewitt
His Ultimate Prize	Maya Blake
More than a Convenient Marriage?	Dani Collins
Second Chance with Her Soldier	Barbara Hannay
Snowed in with the Billionaire	Caroline Anderson
Christmas at the Castle	Marion Lennox
Beware of the Boss	Leah Ashton

HISTORICAL

Not Just a Wallflower	Carole Mortimer
Courted by the Captain	Anne Herries
Running from Scandal	Amanda McCabe
The Knight's Fugitive Lady	Meriel Fuller
Falling for the Highland Rogue	Ann Lethbridge

MEDICAL

Gold Coast Angels: A Doctor's Redemption	Marion Lennox
Gold Coast Angels: Two Tiny Heartbeats	Fiona McArthur
Christmas Magic in Heatherdale	Abigail Gordon
The Motherhood Mix-Up	Jennifer Taylor
The Secret Between Them	Lucy Clark
Craving Her Rough Diamond Doc	Amalie Berlin